## FIRST THERE WAS ~~~~~~ IN THE SKY....

Then *they* had come. M'uri had never seen anything like *them* before. They were not beasts, surely, for they did not look like beasts. They looked almost like the people, but they were not of the people. Their skin was a peculiar color, their manes were strange, and their eyes were not like the eyes of the people. They, too, were colored differently, and they looked lifeless. They did not glow. But most of all—and this she found the most astonishing—she could not sense that they had ever *been* before. They had no Ones Who Were! Surely, then, these were not people. But if they were not beasts, and if they were not people, then what *were* they?

There was no way for M'uri to know that they were humans, but instinct told her that she and her people, the Shades, should fear these strange creatures. And soon that instinct would be proven all too dreadfully right. . . .

# EPIPHANY

## Science Fiction from SIGNET

# Epiphany

*by*
*Nicholas*
*Yermakov*

A SIGNET BOOK
NEW AMERICAN LIBRARY
TIMES MIRROR

Copyright © 1982 by Nicholas Yermakov

SIGNET, SIGNET CLASSICS, MENTOR, PLUME, MERIDIAN AND NAL
BOOKS *are published by The New American Library, Inc.,
1633 Broadway, New York, New York 10019*

FIRST PRINTING, NOVEMBER, 1982

1  2  3  4  5  6  7  8  9

PRINTED IN THE UNITED STATES OF AMERICA

For Keli—
the rest of you guys should be
so lucky

# PROLOGUE

She looked like a beautiful child preserved in sapphire quartz. Her Asian features were delicate, and the gentle contours of her naked body always evoked in Anderson a sexual excitement. Her biological age was twenty-seven, but she looked much younger, like a girl barely in her teens. In strictly chronological terms, she was much older. Old enough to be Anderson's great-great-grandmother.

As he stared down into the cryogen containing Lieutenant Win T'ao "Wendy" Chan, Lowell Anderson told himself he never should have come. He never should have seen her to begin with, certainly not like this. As an impersonal statistic, she would have been much easier to deal with. Until he had seen her, she was not a person, but a "Seedling."

Anderson looked away from the sleeping form of Wendy Chan, down the rows of cryogens in the specially constructed cargo hold of the FTL ship *Blessing*. He kept telling himself that it was ludicrous to feel misgivings. He had made his choice and there would be no turning back. But as he stared down into the cryogen at the face of Wendy Chan, he couldn't help thinking of his granddaughter. Her only sin had been wanting to live forever.

Anderson had never really meant to come aboard the *Blessing*, but some strange curiosity had impelled him to see the Seedlings for himself. They were being kept in storage aboard the ship, being conditioned even as they slept. When they arrived at their destination, they would know what to do. *If* they arrived. That was solely up to Wendy Chan.

The four men who were the Directorate of ColCom were well accustomed to thinking of the people who served under them as pawns in a much larger game than they could understand. A tremendous implication of the Boomerang mission had been overlooked by the members of the survey team.

Indeed, it would not have occurred to people not accustomed to thinking of human lives as being expendable. It had occurred to Anderson.

The Directorate selected pawns. Five thousand of them. They chose them very carefully. The pawns were not aware of the moves that they would be required to make. Their approval had not been necessary, so it had not been asked of them. They were selected and carefully conditioned. They were about to be placed upon the game board.

The *Blessing* was under heavyguard. No one could come aboard save one of the Directors. Only those four men knew what was aboard the *Blessing*. They were the only ones who knew her mission. There was a great deal at stake, and knowing that, Anderson had not been able to resist. He had to come aboard. He had to *see* them, especially Wendy Chan.

He had only meant to make one visit, but he kept coming back. He kept walking down the rows of cryogens, staring at the faces through the sapphire mist, stopping always at the unit containing Wendy Chan.

The *Blessing* was about to depart for Boomerang. It would be Anderson's last visit. He felt a little bit afraid. He wondered if he, too, would be punished for attempting to play God. There were so many things that could go wrong. It was a monumental gamble, but at stake was immortality.

# CHAPTER ONE

Paul Tabarde was several hundred light-years and half a lifetime away from Louisiana. His living quarters aboard orbital station Gamma 127 were a considerable comedown from his fifteen-room conapt overlooking the Bourbon Street atrium in New Orleans. Even his office complex in Cheyenne Mountain was luxurious by comparison. He did not yet know enough about his mission to be a security risk and have his movements restricted, so he had the run of the entire station. Nevertheless, he was accompanied everywhere by an armed guard and did not have access to the sector occupied by the Directorate. It seemed incongruous to him that he should require an armed escort aboard a ColCom base, but he had worked for the service long enough to understand its bureaucratic foibles and petty paranoias. After all, it was his job.

It was not his first time on an orbital station, but it was the first time he had been so far away from Earth. As a specialist in SEPAP, Situational Evaluation and Personnel Adjustive Practices, he had rarely gone off-planet, working mainly at the headquarters complex in Colorado. He had not been "volunteered" for this mission, for his position made him too important. Rather, he had been requested, very politely, to undertake it strictly on a need-to-know basis. The request had come from the Directorate itself.

What the Directors felt he needed to know at that point was very little. It would involve a top-secret assignment, off-planet, with an extended period of time spent working in the field. "How exended?" he had asked. The answer was, "indefinitely."

He had smiled when he heard that word. One thing ColCom really hated was imprecision. One thing ColCom could not totally control was the fallibility of its personnel. It needed someone like him on a mission. The fact that it had asked *him* and not just someone like him meant that the mission was of great importance. What it meant to Paul was that he would be getting a chance to play shrink again. It had been a long time, and he was nothing if not curious. He had hesitated only for a moment before saying he would do it.

The implied challenge in the situation was what had prompted him to voluteer. A flesh-and-blood challenge as opposed to day after day spent sifting through reports and data several generations removed from living, breathing, feeling human beings. He couldn't put a microfiche on a couch. The decision had not been difficult for him to make. He was still young, in his early forties, and he had no family or strong personal involvements. His personal energies had been devoted almost exclusively to his career, and in that he had been very successful. He was rich, he had status and a Council level position in Colonization Command, but in the process of achieving that, he had somehow lost sight of his original vocation, or it had lost sight of him. There had been a minor crisis when he had turned forty, what he later referred to only half jokingly as the I've-got-everything-I've-ever-wanted-so-what-the-hell-is missing blues, but he had been able to accept the responsibility for the direction that his life had taken, understanding that it had been necessary to give up certain things in order to gain others. Yet he had never been able to fully quell the restlessness within him. Now he had a chance to change direction, to break out of the mold again.

He had broken out as far as the bachelor officers' quarters on Gamma 127. He had no idea what came next, but he was fairly certain that it had something to do with the FTL ship *Wanderer*.

It was a psychiatrist's job to listen, and since he had arrived at the station, he had been listening very carefully. A ship called the *Wanderer* was the subject of much speculation. The ship came out of nowhere, stayed long enough to take on supplies, and then departed again for an unknown destination. Rumor had it that this ship was the reason the Directorate had set up temporary headquarters aboard the station. Each time the ship arrived, they went aboard. The crew of the *Wanderer* never left the ship. No one knew who the *Wanderer*'s captain was. She took on no cargo and discharged no freight save for a handful of sealed and classified containers. These were immediately shipped out on a Directorate shuttle, again to an unspecified destination.

Now a new ship had arrived, fresh grist for the rumor

mills and gossip circuits. The two ships were somehow linked, if by nothing more substantial than their common air of mystery. The FTL ship *Blessing* was docked at the station and under constant guard. The base security forces had never been required to play soldier so often or for so long in the past. If there were people aboard the *Blessing*, they were never seen. If the ship carried any cargo, it was unknown. If the ship had any purpose, its mission wasn't listed. And if there were any people aboard Gamma 127 who could relieve the mounting curiosity, they weren't talking.

It was generally accepted that the *Wanderer* was "ghosting," playing games with the collapsed physics of the Hawking drive system. Zone travel enabled her captain to leave the station, spend an unspecified amount of time at his destination—perhaps months, years, or even decades—then return to Gamma 127 within only days or weeks of his departure. The question was, how long was he away, what was he doing, and where was he doing it? No one knew. Tabarde had a feeling he would soon find out.

The *Wanderer* was back.

Jake was waiting in the wardroom of the *Wanderer* when the Directorate came aboard. He was surprised to see that there was someone with them. Usually, the briefing sessions consisted of only himself and the four Directors of Col-Com—Lowell Anderson, the paternal former Senator from Massachusetts; Manfred Hermann, the former Chancellor of the German Republic; Rostislav Malik, the corpulent Russian, late Minister of the KGB; and Sven Jorgensen, the lean Swede who had once run the North Atlantic Conglomerate. The fifth man with them was a tall black civilian who appeared to be in his mid-forties. He was expensively dressed and had a very alert air about him. Anderson performed the introductions.

"Colonel Jake Thorsen, Dr. Paul Tabarde."

They shook hands across the table.

"What's your Ph.D. in, Doctor?" Jake said.

"I'm a psychiatrist."

"Ah."

Anderson chuckled. "Don't worry, Colonel. Your sanity is not in question. At least, not yet."

"I take it that Dr. Tabarde—"

"Paul," said Tabarde.

"Paul . . . is briefed on the mission?"

"Actually, I don't know anything about it," Paul said,

5

"other than that it's very hush-hush and very hot on the gossip circuit. I'm dying to find out what it is."

Jake looked surprised, then glanced at Anderson expectantly.

"Dr. Tabarde is with SEPAP," the Director said. "He will be accompanying you on your return trip."

Jake raised his eyebrows. "SEPAP personnel in the field? Not exactly s.o.p., is it?"

"Nothing about the Boomerang mission is," said Malik.

"Boomerang?" Tabarde frowned, reaching back into his memory. "We've still got a team on Boomerang? I thought the report said—"

"That Boomerang is unsuitable for colonization," Malik finished for him. "Quite correct. That is what the report said."

"I'm afraid I don't understand," said Paul. "Why would we still have a team on Boomerang?"

"Not a survey team, Doctor," said Hermann. "A permanent research installation."

Tabarde leaned back in his chair, a thoughtful expression on his face.

"Okay," he said, "I'll shut up and listen. It seems my need-to-know status is about to be expanded somewhat."

"All the way," said Anderson. "There's no security risk, since you will not be leaving this ship."

"I see." Paul cleared his throat. "I'm afraid that I haven't had a chance to pack my things."

"It's been taken care of," said Anderson.

Tabarde nodded. It was a little late for second thoughts.

"Suppose you brief the doctor, Colonel?" Jorgensen said. "It would be interesting to hear your perspective on the mission."

"And get him started on his shrinking?" Jake said with a smile. "Is that your job on this party, Paul?"

Paul shrugged. "A man's gotta do what a man's gotta do."

Jake grinned. "I think I like you. Okay, here goes. The original survey team sent out to Boomerang discovered a sentient race. Called them Shades."

Tabarde sat forward.

"At first there was some question as to their sentience," Jake said. "The Shades are supra-agrarian, nontribal beings with a strong territorial imperative."

"That seems contradictory," said Paul.

"Yes, doesn't it? They have toolmaking capabilities, yet they don't construct shelters. They possess fairly sophisticated and extensive knowledge of their environment, primarily of an empirical and pragmatic nature with no apparent evidence of any fundamental awareness of more basic biological principles. Yet they have no spoken or written language and do not communicate with one another."

Paul frowned. "That's impossible. How would they acquire the necessary—"

"Wait," said Jake. "I haven't gotten to the good part."

"The good part?"

"They don't die."

Jake sat back and watched Paul. He seemed to be awaiting a reaction.

"You're telling me—"

"That they live forever, yes," said Jake. "Oh, their bodies are capable of death, in the physical sense, but the soul survives. Intact. Aware."

Paul glanced at the Directors, who were watching him with interest.

"He's joking," Paul said.

Anderson shook his head.

"The *soul*?"

"In a manner of speaking," said Malik.

"You have proof of this?"

"We have seen it, Doctor," said Jorgensen.

Paul bit his lower lip, A race of *immortal* beings? *The soul survives?*

"Would it be possible to get a drink aboard this ship?" said Paul.

"Sure," said Jake. "Scotch do?"

"Oh, yes, very well, thank you. I take mine neat."

It took but a moment for Jake to produce a bottle and six glasses.

"Okay," said Paul, after downing a shot. "Now run this past me one more time."

"If you think you're surprised now," said Jake, "wait till you meet Colonel Michaels. I think I'll save that for now, though. Well, let's make a long story short. The Shades are capable of . . . I'm not even sure what the hell to call it. We say psychic transference, and I guess it's as good a term as any. Imagine you're a Shade. Imagine that you're dying. You send out a sort of psychic call. Another Shade responds. There follows something called the Touch."

"As in physically touching someone?"

"Yes, that's involved, but this is a special sort of contact. It produces a merging phenomenon wherein your life force,

7

your personality, your identity or soul, call it what you will, whatever it is that makes you who you are . . . this life essence is transmitted or transferred to the other Shade. Your body dies, but your identity survives intact within that other Shade. It's as if, for example, you and I were to occupy the same body."

"That's incredible."

"There's more. There seems to be no limit to this merging phenomenon. Now here's where it gets a little hard to follow. Imagine that you and I are Shades, that your body has died and I've taken on your life force. You are now within me, your body being the only thing you've left behind. Now we're sharing consciousness in the most literal sense. We have access to each other's thoughts, memories, experience. I know what you know and vice versa. Within the cultural matrix of the Shades, I am known as the One That Is. In other words, I am alive and occupying the body I was born in. You, who have left behind your body to merge with me, are now one of the Ones Who Were."

"*One* of?"

"Exactly. Remember I said there was no limit to this merging. This . . . evolutionary tradition, if you will, goes back God only knows how far. Within each and every individual Shade, insofar as we can call them individuals, there exist literally thousands upon thousands of Ones Who Were. An uncountable number of entities or personalities. But it gets even more complex than that. Evidently, there is a merging *within* the merging. The Ones Who Were act as a conglomerate of living beings, a gestalt, but there is also a gestalt within the gestalt. The survival of the fittest comes into play to a degree here. Every entity survives, but with each merging, there comes another merging within the Ones Who Were. As nearly as I can tell, this is controlled primarily by strength of personality, richness of experience and knowledge, and individual power. Again, the term 'individual' doesn't properly apply here, but we're saddled with certain limitations in terms of our semantics.

"There are certain group identities within the Ones Who Were. Now, somewhere along the line, dominant entities emerged. These dominant entities among the Ones Who Were absorbed other entities so that just as the Ones Who Were are contained within the One That Is, these weaker Ones Who Were become contained within the stronger Ones Who Were. There is no death or negation of identity. It all becomes one happy family with one specific 'entity' achieving dominance.

8

So each physical Shade is, in fact, an entire tribe of entities that are limitless in number. No death. Rather, a continuation with constant augmentation of identity, strength, knowledge, and experience."

Tabarde exhaled slowly. "It's fantastic. But with no written or spoken language, how do they communicate?"

"It seems they once had a spoken language," said Jake, "but they've evolved—or perhaps devolved—to a point where it's no longer used as such. They have vocal apparatus, different from ours, but atrophied. The language is preserved and it continues to be used, but it's only spoken internally, that is, within the One That Is. So there is communication in that sense, between the One That Is and the Ones Who Were, within one body, but there is no communication among the various 'tribes' contained within the different living physical bodies. I don't know if that's really clear. If we were all Shades here, we would all have communication going on within ourselves, communication among the Ones Who Were within each of us and ourselves, but we couldn't talk to each other. A Shade Director Malik would not be able to communicate with a Shade Director Anderson."

"I see."

"That is our main problem in making contact with the Shades," said Jake. "We'd have to deal with only one One That Is at a time. The other problem is that we have no idea what this language of theirs sounds like. Our priority project at Boomerang Base is a speech analyzer program, but we're working blind. Any sound must be heard before it can be imitated. If we could assemble a speech analyzer program, we could couple it with a synthesizer and work with remote hand-held terminals and in that way effect communication. But we have no model. The Shades can't help us to hear those sounds because they no longer make them. And they don't want to help. The Shades avoid us like the plague."

"Given all those problems," said Paul, "how on earth have you managed to learn so much about them?"

Jake smiled. "That's where Colonel Michaels comes in."

"The mission records are all aboard this ship, so you can study them at your leisure," said Anderson, "but to satisfy your immediate curiosity, Shelby Michaels, a member of the original survey team, is currently the most valued member of the project. During the initial mission, she had a Shade merge with her. Within her now exists a multiplicity of alien personalities. In point of fact, she is no longer really human. Not Shade, not human, but a different sort of creature entirely.

9

We have come by most of our knowledge as a result of direct communication with the Shade entities within her, who, having access to her mind and her human vocal cords, are now capable of speaking English."

"Good God," said Paul.

Malik smiled. "You desired a challenge, Doctor. This is the best one we could come up with. A man with your expertise is needed on this project. Also, the men and women on Boomerang are subject to unique pressures and could benefit from an ongoing program of therapy. It is a unique opportunity, but there is a price. The assignment is of indefinite duration."

Paul met Malik's level stare. "I think I undertsand," he said. "You mean I won't be coming back, don't you?"

"You will be returning to Gamma 127 periodically, along with Colonel Thorsen, to report your progress," Anderson said. "We want to monitor this mission very carefully. However, I am afraid that you will most likely not see Earth or any of the colonies again during your lifetime. I'm sorry."

Paul took a moment to digest this. He sighed, then smiled. "That's all right," he said. "It's worth it."

Paul turned off the monitor screen and rubbed his eyes. He was tired, but tremendously excited. He felt like an explorer about to embark into uncharted regions. After the Directors had left, Jake Thorsen had helped him settle into one of the main cabins. He had met some of the crew briefly and all his things had been brought aboard, but he had spent most of his time scanning the records of the Boomerang mission. He had no doubt that he was about to have the greatest experience of his life.

He had studied all the information the mission had gathered about the Shades and their wild planet, but the thing which fascinated him the most was the discovery of what seemed to be a common ground between the phenomenon of the Shades and his own field of study.

Thorsen had referred to group entities among the Ones Who Were, identity gestalts. One detail that had been left for him to discover upon studying the mission records was the role grouping of these gestalt identities. Each of them had specific functions to perform in the life of the One That Is. There was a group entity known as the Great Father, there was a Great Mother, a Great Healer, a Great Hunter, and the Father Who Walked in Shadow.

"Archetypes!" he had said to Thorsen.

10

"How's that?"

Jake had come to his quarters to see how he was settling in, only to find him totally engrossed in the mission records. They discussed Paul's interpretation over drinks.

"I'm talking about Jung's term for the collective unconscious," said Paul excitedly. "He wrote about it during the early twentieth century. It was one of the most controversial aspects of his personality theory. Jung said that the collective unconscious was composed of latent memory traces inherited from racial history, a psychic residue that accumulated with repeated experiences over many generations. Jung argued that it was a universal phenomenon attributable to common evolution."

"I'm afraid I don't follow you, Doc," said Jake. "It's a little over my head."

"All right, let's take fear of the dark, for example," said Paul, warming to the subject. "According to Jung, this was a racial memory, a possibility that man was predisposed to as a result of his primitive ancestors encountering many dangers in the dark. Now, we're talking about a potential inherent in man, a potential for fearing the dark. This possibility might never develop in modern man unless it was strengthened by specific experiences."

"You mean that I might not become afraid of the dark unless something happened to me that would bring out that fear, which is already there?" said Jake.

"The *potential* for it is there," said Paul, "according to Jung. And this potential would make you more susceptible to having such an experience. Here's another example: Every human ever born had a mother. As a result, we're all born with a predisposition to perceive and react to a mother. This predisposition is imprinted upon us by evolution. Jung's theory was that the collective unconscious was the inherited foundation for the entire structure of the personality. The learning process is substantially influenced by the collective unconscious. As he put it, 'The form of the world into which he is born is already inborn in him as a virtual image.' The collective unconscious holds possibilities which are locked away from the conscious mind. It contains all subliminal contents, things which have been overlooked or forgotten and the wisdom and experience of uncounted centuries, all laid down in its archetypal organs. He said that if the wisdom of the collective unconscious was ignored by the ego, it would disrupt the rational processes by taking hold of them and twisting

11

them into distorted forms, from which stemmed phobias, delusions, and so forth."

"But I don't see how the Ones Who Were fit into all of this," Jake said, frowning.

"I was coming to that. The components which make up the collective unconscious have various names: archetypes, dominants, primordial images, and so on. Think of it as a thought form that is imprinted on the brain as a result of evolution. It creates images that correspond to some aspect of the conscious experience. For instance, the archetype of the sun god came about as a result of countless generations being exposed to the sun as a powerful, light-giving, dominating heavenly body which exerted a profound influence on their existence. It was deified and worshiped, giving rise to the whole idea of a supreme being. This idea is easily formed for us now because we're predisposed to it through imprintation and need little reinforcement from our experience to bring it forth into the conscious mind."

"You're saying that the religious fever on Earth didn't just happen as a result of the plague drug? That the idea for it was already there and it only needed the plague drug to act as a stimulus to kick it up into the conscious mind?" said Jake.

"Well, essentially, yes. There are supposed to be numerous archetypes within the collective unconscious. Archetypes of birth, rebirth, death, power, magic, the hero, the demon, the wise old man, the earth mother, the animal, the shadow—"

"The Great Father, the Great Mother, the Great Hunter," said Jake.

"*Exactly!* And these archetypes are not necessarily discrete from one another," said Paul. "They can blend with or merge with each other! Do you see what I'm getting at? What we have discovered is a race of beings with their own living archetypes, each Shade an evolutionary microcosm. The mind simply reels at the implications!"

Paul sat down on the bunk and leaned back against the bulkhead. It really wasn't fair. He was ecstatic at the idea of being able to study the Shades—and Colonel Michaels, what an opportunity she represented!—but the thought of the scientific community at large being excluded from this project was saddening. Once again, the petty paranoias of ColCom were at fault, only this time, Paul thought, they weren't so petty.

The Shades, too, had a god. Theirs was an earth god, the All Father, who they believed lived within the bosom of the All Mother, their term for Boomerang. The irony of the situation was that the Shades were predisposed to conclude, given exposure to the human concept of God, that their god and the god of the humans was the same Supreme Being. They believed that the All Father was, in fact, the human God as well. That the All Father had made humans as they were, incapable of merging, so that their loneliness would cause them to embark upon a search for knowledge that would culminate in their finding the All Mother, where God resided. And for that reason, the discovery of the Shades had to remain a closely guarded secret.

For humans, life flared only briefly, like a match flame, then was extinguished. The striking of a match. A simple parable of life. Perhaps, Paul thought, that was how it had been meant to be. Certainly there were many people on Earth and its colony worlds who believed so now, after the plague drug.

Its original, considerably less colorful name had been batch 235. The scientists who had invented it were more concerned with what it did than with what it should be called. Their field was anti-agathic research, and they were not so much interested in improving the quality of life as they were in prolonging it. The early results with batch 235 had been extremely promising, but it had been a long way from being fully tested and developed. Paul knew only too well that when it came to funding research, people were always less interested in the process than in the promise of quick results. The inventors of batch 235 thought that they might be forgiven if they exaggerated somewhat in their claims of what the drug would do when they announced it to the media. They thought that given enough time, they would at least come close enough to their projected goal to satisfy the masses. It was a shame that no one had ever told them that the masses are never satisfied. As it happened, they were not given enough time. And they were not forgiven.

The necessary funds came through and work continued, but people were impatient. Where was the "immortality pill"? The imaginative men and women of the media had so christened batch 235, taking the somewhat exaggerated claims made by the scientists who had developed it and exaggerating them still further. Who could blame them? Who wouldn't want to live forever, especially when told that there was a drug that would enable them to do so? Those who controlled it had insisted that it wasn't ready, that they needed more time and money for research. Or, perhaps, were they suddenly reluctant to part with their secret? More than a few of the media had made that suggestion. Following the ancient law that wherever there arises a demand, there must come an outlet of supply, the formula was stolen and the drug began to appear on the black market. It was expensive, but what was life worth, after all?

The immortality pill, which was not a pill at all but a program consisting of a long series of painful injections, proved impossible to control. And in time, it became gruesomely apparent that the drug was not all that it had appeared to be at first. And then it received a new name. Plague drug.

The drug did prolong the life span, but at an awful price. The changes wrought in the body chemistry resulted in a massive number of birth defects. Monster babies. Paul knew several people who had given birth to "plague children." There was one in Director Anderson's family. Anderson's granddaughter had not survived the childbirth, which had been fortunate for her, because those who had taken the treatments died in agony, victims of their own body chemistry run amok. The situation was widespread. The drug had been smuggled out to many of the colony worlds, as well.

In the aftermath of the tragedy, there came about a massive religious revival, and people came to believe that what had happened to them was a punishment from God. They were told by fervent preachers that the Creator had not meant for any of His creatures to enjoy eternal life, and they believed it. Death could not be banished. No one would survive. Only the Directorate of ColCom knew otherwise, thought Paul. And now, so did he.

On Earth and throughout its colonies, there were vast numbers of hideously deformed people, plague children who had survived the high mortality rate. They existed as constant, living reminders of the fallibility of man. There were still many victims of the plague drug who had survived long past the normal life expectancy, survived as walking time bombs, never knowing when the drug would take its inevitable toll. What would their reaction be, Paul wondered, if they were to learn that there was a race of beings who lived forever? How would they react if they knew that this immortal race believed in God, that this same God who had inflicted a plague upon humanity for attempting to achieve immortality had bestowed the gift upon a race of aliens who were little more than animals? Paul could see the preachers screaming their defiance, blaming Satan, bringing down hellfire and damnation and stirring to a boil a stew the like of which had not been seen since the days of witch burning and the Spanish Inquisition. Damn their God to hell, thought Paul. Already there was a large faction which fought for the cessation of space travel. It was insane. If God had meant for Man to travel to the stars, he would have placed men there. If God had meant for Man to fly, he would have given him wings. If God had meant for Man to think, he would not have given him priests.

In one way, at least, the Directorate was no different. They were afraid, and so they had classified the momentous discovery, harkening back to the old bromide that there are some things that man was not meant to meddle with, some things he was not meant to know. Paul was elated by the discovery, excited that he was to play a part in it, but he despaired because he would not have the opportunity to share it. Scientists could make discoveries, but the ignorant were the ones who would rule upon them. Paul lay back upon the bunk and tried to get some rest. *Plus ça change, plus c'est la même chose.*

## CHAPTER TWO

The *Wanderer* was under way. Thorsen had been anxious to start back. There had been a delay, but he had grown accustomed to bureaucratic red tape over the years. He gently eased the ship away from the orbital station.

"I notice the *Blessing* is gone," said Paul.

Thorsen gave him a blank look.

"I had assumed the *Blessing* had something to do with our mission," Tabarde said by way of explanation.

"Why's that?" said Jake.

"There was quite an air of mystery about the ship back at the station," Paul said. "As there was about the *Wanderer*."

Thorsen shrugged. "It would stand to reason that our project is not the only one that's classified. The Directorate are making Gamma their temporary headquarters. There are probably all sorts of top-secret goings-on at that base these days."

"You don't seem very curious," Paul said.

Jake chuckled. "Hell, I used to be their flight jockey. Attached to the Directorate as their own personal pilot. When I first pulled the duty, I was thrilled to death until I found out that most of my job would consist of flying a desk. Personally, I think they'd classify their shorts if they could. And who's to say they can't?"

"I take it that you much prefer what you're doing now, then?" said Paul.

"Absolutely. I'm a spacer. This is where I belong. I'll tell you, though, I'd just about given up on it until this mission came along. I'm not a young man anymore, and I would have been due for retirement in a few years. I didn't think much of my chances of getting to command a working ship again, much less going on a field mission. Now they can't retire me. I know too much." He laughed.

"How did it happen that you became involved?" said Paul.

"By accident," Jake said. "When the original Boomerang survey team returned, they put out a call for volunteers for a top-secret detail. I thought it might be an honest-to-God mission, so I volunteered. Turned out the detail involved pulling security duty. I had to baby-sit Colonel Shelby Michaels while she was at Gamma."

"I see. You know, I've been very curious about her. What is she like?"

"I think you'll have to judge that for yourself," said Jake. He grinned. "You have some surprises coming."

"I'm looking forward to them. By the way, when will we be returning to Gamma? Are we on some sort of timetable?"

"Roughly speaking. We'll be coming back to Gamma in about a year's time, for us. It will be something like a week or two for them, though."

Paul shook his head. "I understand ghosting in theory, but I can't get used to it in practice. Is there such a thing as Zone lag?"

Jake laughed. "You'll get used to it."

"Mmmm. I've often wondered what it would be like to push your chances, to use the collapsed physics of the Hawking drive system to travel back into the past and meet yourself. It poses a fascinating riddle."

Jake nodded. "You're not alone, Doc. It's something every spacer's thought about at one time or another. The grandfather paradox. What would happen if you could travel back into the past and meet your own grandfather before he married your grandmother and kill him? Then your father would never have been born, which would mean you could never be born, so how could you have gone back and killed your granddad in the first place?"

"I'm almost curious enough to want to try it," Paul said.

"Well, you know what they say about curiosity."

"What's it like to pilot a ghosting ship?"

"You sure ask a lot of questions, don't you?" Jake said.

"You don't want to talk about it."

"I'd rather not."

"Every Zone pilot I've ever met has always refused to describe the experience," Paul said. "They've never told me why."

Jake hesitated.

"We can drop it, if you like."

"I'll tell you what, Doc," Jake said. "I'll try to explain why we don't like to talk about it, but I won't tell you what it's like in the Zone. All right?"

"Sure."

"I can understand your wanting to know," Jake said. "You like to know what makes people tick. The fact is, Zone pilots don't like to talk about ghosting because it's a very personal thing. It's scary. I guess you can say we're superstitious about it. The experience is different for every individual. How many times have you been aboard a ghosting ship?"

"This will be my third FTL voyage."

"Well, I've done it many, many times, and the odds of losing it go up each time you do it. When a ship goes through the Zone, you're in coldsleep, along with everyone else aboard. The pilot is the only one awake. That, in itself, can get to you. The anticipation. There comes a moment when you dive into the Zone when you confront your own existence, your own reality, in the most direct way possible. You'd better have it straight about what's real, otherwise . . ."

"Otherwise . . . what?" Paul said.

Jake shook his head. "I don't know. And I'm not anxious to find out."

"I wish I knew what it was like."

"Careful, Doc. Your profession's showing."

Paul smiled. "I know. I can't help it."

"I've got a guy I'd like you to meet," Jake said. "Name's Drew Fannon. He was on the original survey team, along with Nils Björnsen and Shelby Michaels. The two of you should have some pretty interesting dscussions. Fannon's not the sort of man you run into very often these days. Physically, he's almost young enough to be my son. Chronologically, he's old enough to be my grandfather several times over."

"A pre-FTL sleeper," Paul said.

Jake nodded. "FTL came about while he was on the Boomerang mission. The survey ship was sublight-drive. They don't make 'em like Fannon anymore. It's a funny thing—the idea of Zone travel really bothers him, but the thought of what he used to do, dreaming away entire lifetimes during sublight voyages, never having a firm sense of time to hold onto, moving like a corpse through an ever-changing universe ... that takes a kind of strength I don't think I have."

"It sounds as if you have a great deal of respect for him," Paul said.

Jake smiled. "I used to read about people like him when I was just a kid. Time's passed him by, in more ways than one. Not that he cares."

"What about the other member of the original team, Nils Björnsen? What do you think of him?"

"Ah, now we're talking about the opposite side of the coin," said Jake. "They're both coldsleep spacers, but that's about where the similarity ends. Fannon's a hard man, tough, uncompromising, self-sufficient. Nils is, well, I hesitate to say softer, but that's the word that springs to mind. I'm not saying that he's soft, you understand—"

"Just that he's the gentler of the two," said Paul.

"Yes. Nils is a thoughtful man. Fannon is a brooder. Jeez, seems like I'm doing your job for you, Doc. You haven't even met these people yet and already you're digging."

"I'm anxious," said Paul. "I guess it shows. You know, this whole thing is making me feel years younger. I feel as I did when I just got out of medical school and had it all before me."

Jake nodded. "I can understand that. I felt that way when I found out I was going on this mission."

"I notice that you refer to Fannon by his last name and to Captain Björnsen by his first," said Paul.

Jake shrugged. "Nothing in that, really. Everyone calls Fannon by his last name. Only one who calls him Drew from time to time is Shelby."

"I see."

"You do, huh?"

"I gather the two of them are very close?" said Paul.

"Yeah. You might say that."

18

"Am I making you feel you're talking out of school?"

"No, not really," said Jake. He paused. "Yeah, A little."

"Why?"

"I think you'd better pursue that line of questioning with Fannon."

"All right. I will. Can we talk about the Shades?"

"We can talk about anything you like, Doc. It's just that I don't much like to talk about other people's relationships. I don't really know the story, you understand?"

"Of course."

"What about the Shades?"

"I've been studying the mission records," said Paul. "There are quite a number of things I find very interesting, but one thing stands out. This 'empathic projection' phenomenon. Can you tell me about it?"

"Yeah, I can. You'll experience it for yourself, but if you're not used to it, it could throw you. It's something that sneaks up on you. I've never been able to pinpoint when it begins, but I'm aware of feeling it after a while. I don't believe the Shades do it consciously. Shelby says they don't. The Ones Who Were within her claim that they didn't know about it until they merged with Shelby. However, I don't think that necessarily means that other Shades are the same way."

"How do you mean?" said Paul.

"Well, we have people with esper abilities, don't we? Some people are aware of having them, in other people it's latent, and most of us haven't got it at all, right?"

"I see what you mean. Go on."

"Well, the records don't really have anything concrete on it because we really don't know much about it at this point. I think it works something like an esper potential. It would make sense from several standpoints. First of all, all evidence we have indicates that their ability to merge with each other is a psychic function. Also, among the Ones Who Were is a group entity called the Father Who Walked in Shadow."

"Yes, I find that especially interesting," said Paul.

"Well, in that case, you'll be wanting to have a talk with T'lan," said Jake.

"Who is T'lan?"

"Shelby's Shadow entity."

"I'll actually be able to *speak* with him?"

"With *them*," Jake said. "Remember, it's a group entity. But we all use individual address forms in referring to the Ones Who Were. They understand that it's more convenient

19

for us that way. Anyway, T'lan, he's kind of hard to describe. I don't think I'll try. I wouldn't want to prejudice you in any way. The point I'm trying to make is that what makes T'lan the entity he-they are is similar to what makes some people espers and others not. I'll tell you a little story to illustrate the point.

"I was out beyond the base perimeter with Shelby one day. You know about Sturmann poles? We use them to set up a field around the base for protection. Well, we were out in the brush, beyond it, just the two of us. A hellhound surprised us."

"I haven't gotten to the wildlife on Boomerang yet," said Paul. "I've mostly been scanning the personnel records and such. What is a hellhound?"

"A particularly nasty sort of creature," Jake said. "Its name pretty much describes it. It looks a lot like a big dog with a bad temper. A *really* big dog. Say, about the size of a Terran lion."

"That's a very big dog," said Paul.

"It certainly is. They have large fangs and huge talonlike claws that could rip you open with one easy swipe. Boomerang's teeming with them. They're the Shades' principal prey and vice versa. The hellhounds are omnivorous and they'll attack just about anything that moves. They're very strong and very, very fast."

"Well, that's one encounter I'll try to avoid," said Paul.

"We all feel pretty much the same way, although we do form hunting parties and go after them every once in a while," said Jake. "Their meat tastes pretty good. Anyway, we weren't hunting them this time; there were just the two of us. This time, one of them was hunting us. Shades are very sensitive, so Shelby is too, but a hellhound can surprise even a Shade. This one dropped down on us from a tree. It got me first. All things considered, I was pretty lucky. It knocked me to the ground, but I wasn't hurt too badly."

Jake opened his shirt and displayed huge claw marks that were reminders of the incident, deep scars in his left shoulder. Paul winced.

"Shelby was armed," said Jake. "She had a gun and she was carrying a spear, just as the Shades do. The gun stayed in her holster. She didn't use the spear. She just stared the thing down."

"How?"

"*That's* a hell of a good question," Jake said. "I think I know, but it's just a theory. Something like this empathic projection thing. Her T'lan aspect took over. The Father Who Walked in Shadow. She was still Shelby, but I've never seen her look that way before or since. She was like an animal, a very dangerous animal. Seeing her that way made the little hairs on the back of my neck stand up. It was scary, Doc. And it scared the hellhound, too. They just stood there, staring at each other for several seconds, the hellhound growling back in its throat, Shelby not making a sound. And the damn thing backed off. Ran off into the woods. I'll never forget it."

"And you think that her T'lan aspect used some form of psychic projection on the beast?"

"That's just a guess," said Jake. He shrugged. "But it's the best one I've got."

"Why didn't she simply shoot the beast?" said Paul.

"Because it was standing on my chest," said Jake. "Could've been a little messy if it didn't die right away."

Paul swallowed hard. He cleared his throat uneasily. "Yes, well . . . I think I'll go and do some more studying, if you don't mind."

"Sure thing. Let me know if you've got any questions."

"Yes, I . . . I'll do that."


It was time.

Jake quickly double-checked the cryogens, to make sure that all the members of the small crew were properly in alpha coldsleep, their brains held in a thought-free stasis as they slept dreamlessly. Dreams had a reality all their own. Jake wanted to make sure that his would be the only reality within the Zone.

Every time he saw people in coldsleep, it always struck him that they didn't look as if they were sleeping. They looked dead to him. And the cryogens resembled coffins with transparent lids, revealing the mist-shrouded corpses within, giving them a cyanotic, ghostly aspect. He stared down at Paul Tabarde's face. Despite an outward show of insouciance, Tabarde had been nervous entering the cryogen. Some people never get over it, thought Jake. Fannon had spent most of his chronological life in cryogens, and he hated coldsleep.

He liked Tabarde. The man was perhaps overeager, wanting to assimilate everything at once, but that was understandable. Until they had met, Paul Tabarde had known nothing about the mission. Yet he had volunteered for it. That in itself gave Jake a clue as to his personal situation. He smiled. Spending time with the man made his personality rub off on you.

Now he was playing shrink. What would make a man volunteer for a top-secret assignment off-planet that he knew nothing about? The same thing that had made him volunteer for the top-secret detail that had turned out to be security for the members of the returning Boomerang survey team.

Tabarde had not been happy with SEPAP. After spending some time with him, Jake thought he knew why. Sometimes people set goals for themselves that were unrealistic, not in terms of their ability to attain them, but in terms of their suitability. Paul Tabarde was no more suited to a desk job than he was. They were both adventurers, in different respects. Outer space was Jake's special province, inner space was Tabarde's. Just as the *Wanderer* was about to dive into the vortex known to spacers as the Twilight Zone, so did Tabarde long to penetrate the vortex of the unconscious mind. Each held its own dangers, each its own attraction.

Jake left the cryogen banks and went to his flight couch, strapping himself in. The *Wanderer* was now hurtling toward the departure point at almost the speed of light. The massive observation port was shielded. He would have seen nothing of any consequence at this speed anyway. The ship was committed to its course. If there were any errors, it was too late to fix them now.

Ahead of him were four powered asteroids upon which had been constructed the massive Hansen magnets which made the Zone possible. Each manned asteroid was responsible for an awesome task—moving a quantum black hole. When properly aligned, four of them in formation equidistant from each other created an area in the center where their radii intersected, an area of calm where their gravity was canceled out, much as an iron ball with four magnets placed at points equidistant from it would not move. Within this area could be found the Twilight Zone, a vortex where all physical laws broke down. The ship, moving under the full power of its Hawking drive, had to penetrate the exact center of that area to gain access to the Zone. Collapsed physics, unreality, nonexistence. The ship would journey to oblivion. Only the will of its pilot could allow it to survive.

In a vortex where reality did not exist, Jake had to create his own. This was the one drawback of the FTL technology. The vortex did not tolerate reality where none existed. It rejected it. In order to get the ship to Boomerang, Jake had to concentrate, using all his willpower to focus his mind upon the reality that was Boomerang and his experience there. In order for him to do this, he had to have been at his destination before, to have seen it, felt it, assimilated and been a part of it. In order to use Zone travel to get to a destination, at some point a ship using standard drive had to have gone there first, so that the next time, using Zone travel, someone could ghost the ship there in a fraction of the amount of time that a ship using standard sublight drive could make the journey. So there was still a need for coldsleep ships, but there were very few of them and most spacers never met the atavistic loners who were their pilots. In most cases, they were clinically insane. Shelby Michaels had been one of them, before she had transcended her humanity.

It was dangerous to think too much about the metaphysics of ghosting. One of the reasons Zone pilots refrained from talking about it was that no one really knew if the Zone was simply rejecting their reality or if they were creating reality anew each time, literally bringing the universe into a new existence. Playing God. It was a frightening thought and a terrifying concept. In theory, once within the Zone, a ghosting pilot had control of time. In theory, he could return to his home world, at the time of his birth or to any point in his past, at any time. The temptation to play at omnipotence within the Zone was very great. To minimize it, each Zone pilot went through a long conditioning process in a cryogen, a process wherein training was reinforced, powers of concentration and will were strengthened, regulations regarding Zone travel forcibly imprinted. Still, there had been accidents. Ships had entered the Zone never to be heard from again. Such ships were then listed in the records as "ghosts."

What had happened to them? Had their pilots failed in maintaining concentration, causing themselves and their ships and crew to lose reality, thereby ceasing to exist? Were they still somehow trapped within the vortex for all eternity? Or had there been some error in their perception of reality? Did the ships, in fact, emerge from the Zone into some other universe, one of their pilots' own creation? There were rumors in the fleet, rumors that in order to find out the answers to such overwhelming questions ColCom had sent ships out to see what possibilities existed in the Zone, to see if there *were* other universes, if there was a possibility of creating them if there were not. Such rumors surfaced in wardroom discussions and in bars in ports of liberty when drinks had been consumed. Pilots never took part in such discussions, and if pilots were present, such discussions quickly ceased.

Jake relaxed and shut his eyes, took several deep breaths, and began to concentrate. He formed a picture of his destination in his mind. He thought of Boomerang, a planet in the system of a type G yellow dwarf. A planet with a diameter of 15,120.724 kilometers, with a gravity of .75, three-quarters Earth specific. It had one large continent, approximately 138,000 square kilometers, formed by a collision of two smaller landmasses some 15 million years ago. The collision had formed a massive mountain range down the center of the continent rising to heights of 60,000 meters. He thought of the moon which gave Boomerang its name, a body shaped vaguely like a crescent which tumbled across the skies of Boomerang, rising and setting several times in one night, due to its low, fast orbit. He thought of hurricanes and severe storms, most of which headed out to sea, but some of which went inland and caused tremendous damage. With a less severe axial tilt than Earth, Boomerang had more temperate weather overall, although it was hot in the desert region at its equatorial belt. Seasons were of more uniform length, there was no snow, and precipitation was divided fairly equitably among the seasons.

Images of Boomerang flashed through Jake's mind, images of tall and slender trees, animals and flying creatures, flowering grass with yellow blades and purple blooms . . . and Shades. He thought of the tall, slender, beautiful beings, humanoid in appearance, with pearl-gray skin and thick, snowy manes, and cats' eyes that shimmered with a stark violet glow. He thought of Fannon, Nils, and Shelby, the other men and women at Boomerang Base, the base itself, prefabricated buildings in a compound cleared of the heavy jungle growth, an isolated island of modern human technology in a sea of harsh, alien wilderness. He ran through the recent events just before he left, to get a fix in time.

The *Wanderer* stabbed into the vortex. The ship dissolved around him.


It was the most terrifying thing that had ever happened to her, but she could not feel afraid. As the *Blessing* passed into the Twilight Zone, it ceased to exist. During the moment of entry, there had been a sudden vertiginous feeling and then the bottom dropped out, not only the bottom, but the top and sides as well, and Wendy was left dangling in the void, with no perception of her body or surroundings, only an awareness of her self that threatened to fragment into thousands of tiny particles that would spin crazily to nowhere like brilliant shards of shattered glass.

It was her first experience of the Zone. She had been

trained as a coldsleep spacer originally, but she had been prepared as thoroughly as possible for her first excursion through the Zone, prepared by the most extensive and exhausting coldsleep conditioning program any human had ever been subjected to. Her powers of concentration had been strengthened, her fears and insecurities inhibited; she had been programmed with the imperative to get her ship and crew to their destination, with the imperative to survive.

Foremost in her mind as she fought for substance where there was none was all the information that had been programmed into her, a scenario composed of data and computer graphics translated into images within her mind. It was a scenario arrived at through estimation of glacier positions in the mountains of Boomerang, degree of erosion on its coasts, the size of its polar icecaps, and the stellar position relative to its vicinity. She was going back through time, farther than any spacer had gone before. The sense impressions she retained as a member of the original Boomerang survey team helped to guide her through the vortex, but these sense impressions had been modified, certain elements inhibited in favor of the scenario of Boomerang's past.

Inhibited were all her memories of the survey team itself and her experiences as a member of that team. She did not remember the ship that brought them to the planet. She did not remember the fellow members of her team. She did not remember the incident which had resulted in her withdrawal into catatonia, a state from which she had not revived until the condition had been cured by ColCom physicians. She remembered none of this. Instead, the images and sense impressions she had retained, those which had been reinforced by the conditioning process, were the images of Boomerang itself, of its flora and its fauna, of its environment and topography. She had been conditioned to believe that she belonged there, that it was her home.

She seemed to feel a pulling sensation, as though the lack of substantial reality within the Zone exerted a force upon her, a force meant to restore conformity of nonbeing in the Zone by pulling her apart. She resisted, holding on with all her force of will to her self, to what was real, and then there was a cataclysmic sound, a crackling as of a thousand electrical discharges and a shaking all around her as reality and unreality collided, repelling one another and spitting her forth out of the Zone. The ship reappeared around her. The stars were different.

She heard a chiming coming from her console and she

switched on the monitors in the cargo hold, seeing the dome lids of the cryogens retracting, the mist within them dissipating, their occupants reviving, slowly beginning to sit up and move around, attempting to dispel the effects of coldsleep. The Seedlings were awake.

She brought the *Blessing* into orbit around Boomerang. It was a beautiful world, an untouched pastoral planet, one with a harsh environment, but an environment that they had all been trained to feel at home in. They would be the first humans to set foot upon it. There would not be others for at least a thousand years.

# CHAPTER THREE

Paul's first impression was that he had arrived at a resort. A rather primitive resort, but a resort nonetheless. Boomerang Base was situated in the northern hemisphere of the planet, fairly far inland and within several days' travel of the gargantuan mountain range that ran down the center of the continent. The view was spectacular.

The base covered approximately fifty acres of cleared land and was surrounded on all sides by heavy jungle. All around the base perimeter, Sturmann poles had been erected to set up a field that would repel any animal intruders. Boomerang Base looked, incongruously, like an old campus of a small university. The prefabricated buildings were not very large, the tallest of them being only five stories high, and they were arranged in a roughly circular pattern, with the smaller laboratory buildings on the inside. The center of the compound was where the recreational building was situated, which also held the mess hall, kitchens, and library. The men and women of Boomerang Base had worked hard to make this a home. They had used the local flora to create miniature parks and gardens among the buildings. The flowering grass of Boomerang was everywhere, and there were small groves of slender trees. They had even diverted a nearby stream, re-routing it to run through the base compound. It was a lovely place.

Paul was first taken to his room in the dormitory building, then to his office in the central laboratory complex. There he was met by Nils Björnsen, an amiable blond Scandinavian with an easygoing manner and a soft voice. Nils looked less like a survey officer than a college professor.

"Dr. Tabarde, welcome. Good to have you with us," he said, giving Paul a firm handshake.

"Thank you. And please call me Paul."

"I trust you've had a chance to study the mission records on your trip out " said Nils.

"Yes, but not completely. Still, I'm tremendously excited at the prospect of working with you people. I find the Shades absolutely fascinating."

"So do we," said Nils. "We'll try to get you settled in as quickly as possible, make the transition painless. If there's anything you need, please don't hesitate to ask. If we can provide it, it's yours for the asking. We still have some time before third mess—I trust you'd like to get back to your quarters and unpack."

"Actually, I can do that later," Paul said. "What I'd like right now is a tour of the base, if that would be possible."

"Certainly. I'll take you around myself."

"When will I be meeting Colonel Michaels?"

Nils smiled. "Yes, I thought you would be anxious to see her. She's over in the computer lab right now, working on the speech analyzer program. Shall we start there?"

"Please."

As they walked over to the computer lab, Paul tried to keep from overwhelming Nils with questions. He was only partially successful.

"How many people do you have here?"

"Seventy-three, including yourself," said Nils. "Of those, Fannon, Shelby, and I were part of the original survey team, some forty-five came with Jake Thorsen on our return trip to establish the base, and the rest came in on subsequent trips."

"All of them are . . . assigned here for the duration." It was a statement rather than a question.

"Yes."

"How do they feel about that?" said Paul.

"I won't speak for the others," said Nils, "but I've resigned myself to it. I don't feel bitter, if that's what you're getting at. Technically, I suppose you could say that we're all exiles, but

27

I choose not to look at it that way. We have been given a tremendous opportunity to study the most fascinating race humanity has ever come across. In many ways, what we're doing here is no different from what any number of survey missions that I've been on do, only we're set up far more comfortably here. We have more people, we have all the amenities, and we have our work. Look around you. This is a beautiful place. A virgin planet, unspoiled by technology. If I had been given a choice between settling down here and in Luna City, for example, it would have been a very easy choice to make. I like it here."

"It does seem to be a paradise," said Paul, nodding in agreement.

"I would not go quite that far," said Nils. "It is, after all, a primitive planet with a harsh environment. We're all fairly safe inside the compound, but make no mistake, it's rough out in the bush. Don't take it into your mind to go on any solitary nature hikes. Chances are excellent you won't return."

"I'll keep that in mind."

They entered the lab building and walked a short stretch down the hall until they came to a door marked "Heuristics." Even before they opened the door, they could hear a loud, gravelly voice berating someone from within.

" . . . *put up with this absurdity! I'm an engineer, for God's sake. How the hell do you people expect me to function under these circumstances?*"

Nils grinned. "I see Dr. McEnroe is in rare form this evening." He pushed open the door.

A husky middle-aged Irishman with tight, curly hair was standing over someone who was obscured by the computer console. He looked up at their entrance and scowled belligerently, jamming his hands into the pockets of his laboratory whites.

"*More* distractions! How do you expect me to work with these constant interruptions? Here I am, attempting to perform the task of Sisyphus with this fucking program, and every fifteen minutes someone sticks their head in here to see how I'm doing! Get out!"

"Calm down, Sean, you'll burst a blood vessel," Nils said.

"I wouldn't be surprised! And *then* what are you going to do? Where else are you going to find someone idiot enough to construct a program without a model? Do you even realize how many *possibilities* there are? I'm surprised at you, Björnsen, I thought you were one of the rational ones."

"I think our new base psychiatrist will decide that," Nils said. "I wanted you to meet him. This is Dr. Paul Tabarde, late of SEPAP. Dr. Tabarde, Sean McEnroe."

"God help us, they sent us a headshrinker. I could have used another systems analyst."

"Doctor . . ." Paul held out his hand.

McEnroe grunted, came over, and grudgingly shook hands with him. The person seated at the console stood up in full view, and Paul found himself struck speechless.

"Don't mind Sean, doctor," she said, "he's going through male menopause. I'm Shelby Michaels. Welcome to Boomerang."

From a distance, Shelby Michaels looked completely human, except for her thick mane of snow-white hair and glowing violet eyes. As he approached her, Paul could see that her skin was not quite flesh-colored. It had a silvery-blue sheen to it, not quite the pearl-gray color of the Shades, but not human flesh tone, either. It was a moment before he noticed that she was holding out her hand and waiting for him to take it.

"I—I beg your pardon," Paul said, feeling flustered. "I fear I was staring. Somehow, I hadn't expected—"

"It's quite all right, Doctor," she said. "Your reaction is perfectly understandable."

"I'm sorry, Paul," said Nils, "I thought you knew. Didn't Jake tell you?"

"Well, yes, he told me that Colonel Michaels was . . ." He didn't want to say "wasn't entirely human."

"But he neglected to mention my appearance," Shelby finished for him. "That sounds like Jake."

"Somehow, I had assumed that the merging phenomenon was merely a psychic effect," said Paul. "I had no idea . . ."

"You're right there, Doctor," Shelby said. "What you see before you is the result of an unforeseen side effect of Zone travel. I brought the *Wanderer* through on its initial trip to Boomerang. Jake's theory was that I would be best suited to pilot the ship through the Zone because I had firmer ties with Boomerang as a result of the merging. However, none of us anticipated this." She made a gesture toward herself.

"How did it happen?"

"I can't explain the effect, if that's what you mean. All I can tell you is that my being merged with the Ones Who Were must have had something to do with it. My perception of reality is not quite that of a human being."

Paul refrained from reacting to that statement. She did not

29

think of herself as being human? He wanted to pursue that, but it was not the proper time.

She took his silence as embarrassment. "Really, Doctor, no need to concern yourself. I know that seeing me must have been a shock. You should have seen how Jake and Fannon reacted when it happened."

"Yes, well, we won't bother you and Sean," said Nils. "I'm just giving Paul a quick run around the base before third mess. You'll all have time to get acquainted later. If you'll excuse us . . ."

"Yes, *some* of us have work to do," groused McEnroe.

He met Fannon at third mess. He was sitting at a table with Shelby and Nils when Jake and Fannon came over with their trays to join them.

"So you're the shrink?" said Fannon.

"I'm the shrink," said Paul.

"What's the matter, Jake, you tell Anderson we're cracking up out here?"

"I told them that a certain Captain Fannon was in dire need of psychiatric care," said Jake. "Knowing how vital you are to the project, they sent one of their top men from SEPAP."

"Yes, I heard you were one of the Cheyenne Mountain boys," said Fannon.

"News travels fast," Paul said.

"That's 'cause we don't get much. Hey, maybe we should put out a base newstape. The Boomerang Evening Bulletin. Keep everybody posted on all the late-breaking stories, the sports scores—"

"*What* sports?" said Jake.

"So we'll organize a softball team. We can play visiting Shades."

"*Are* there visiting Shades?" said Paul.

"No," said Fannon. "They don't seem to like the neighborhood."

"What Fannon's saying is that we haven't been very succesful in establishing contact with them," Nils said. "Some of them observe us from time to time, but we've not been able to approach them."

"We did make a breakthrough a while back," said Fannon sourly, "for all the good it's done us."

Paul noticed that Nils glanced sharply at Fannon and Shelby stiffened, almost imperceptibly.

"*What* breakthrough?" said Jake. "Nobody mentioned anything about a breakthrough."

"Why, it's simple, Jake," said Fannon. "If you want to get a rise out of the Shades, all you have to do is fall flat on your face."

"I really don't think this is the proper time—" began Nils, but Shelby interrupted him.

"Let him talk, Nils," she said.

"See, it happened while you were away, Jake," Fannon said. There was an unpleasant edge to his voice. "I was out one night, just getting some cool air and smoking a cigarette. Most everybody else was sleeping, except for a few people in the labs. I haven't been sleeping all that well lately, and I sometimes like to take a walk inside the perimeter. You taking notes, Doctor? Anyway, I felt a Shade nearby. I started to pick up on those vibes they send out, and, sure enough, there was one just beyond the field, staring at me. Well, I wasn't in much of a mood to be spied on, so I yelled something or other and threw my cigarette at the Shade. It never would've hit him, of course, because of the field, but that's not the point. The point is, I tripped over a root and fell. Guess what happened next? While I was lying there, feeling like a prize idiot, the Shade got down and stretched out on the ground too! At first, I didn't understand, but then it hit me. *The Ritual of Prayer!*"

"Well, I'll be . . ." said Jake.

"I'm afraid I don't follow," Paul said.

"Shades lie down upon the ground to pray, Paul," Shelby said.

"Of course," said Paul. "They believe that their All Father resides within this planet. The Shade thought Fannon was praying to its god."

"Precisely," Fannon said, watching Shelby.

"It's a way of making contact," Paul said. "Congratulations."

"You're a little premature," said Fannon. "It *would* be a way of making contact, *if* we were given an opportunity to try it."

"What's stopping you?"

"Why don't you ask the Ones Who Were? I hear you've been looking forward to talking to them," Fannon said.

Paul glanced at Shelby. He felt confused, but he tried not to let it show. There was more happening at the table than met the eye, and he was not yet at a point where he could tell the players without a scorecard. There was a tension between Fannon and Shelby, and it seemed to be concerned with something more than just the subject under discussion. He decided to play it by ear. He had little choice.

"How does one go about doing that?" he said.

"One simply asks, Doctor," Shelby said. Only it wasn't Shelby anymore.

Nothing about her had changed, physically, but Paul had seen enough cases of split personality to know that suddenly he was no longer talking to the same person. Her tone of voice, her bearing and manner of speaking, her body language, all had changed in an instant. Paul had the impression that she had somehow grown much older.

"I am K'itar, Dr. Tabarde. The Great Father of the Ones Who Were."

"How do you do?" said Paul cautiously.

"We are unhappy," said K'itar. "We are saddened by the resentment Drew Fannon bears us."

"Why does he resent you?" Paul said.

"There is more to his resentment than he will admit," K'itar said. "We know from Shelby that you are a human Healer. It is our hope that you will help him."

"Stick to the point," said Fannon.

"Very well," K'itar said. "Fannon is correct in his observation that the Ritual of Prayer is a potential means of making contact with the people. Shelby knew this, even before he came to this conclusion as a result of his accident."

"Tell him why she never brought it up," said Fannon.

"I could not allow it," said K'itar. "The All Father has brought humans here as a test to impose upon the people, whom you call Shades. It is for them to undergo this test. They do not yet perceive how great the All Father truly is, just as we did not perceive it until we merged with Shelby and she became the One That Is. They must discover this for themselves. Fannon does not agree. He is impatient. That is what I have observed the most in humans. I do not say this in rebuke, but nevertheless, it is a truth."

"That doesn't—"

"Please, Fannon," said Paul. "Let me. K'itar, don't you think it possible that the All Father also meant this as a test for humans? If humans are here, then couldn't it be argued that the All Father meant for our two races to come in contact? I'll grant you that humans are impatient, but then we don't have as much time as you do."

"This is true," K'itar said, "but there is yet another reason

32

why the Ones Who Were are in disfavor of Fannon's suggestion. He has blasphemed."

Paul noticed that everyone within earshot had stopped eating and talking and was listening carefully to the exchange.

"Blasphemed?" he said. "Against the All Father? How?"

"The Ritual of Prayer is a holy thing," the Great Father said. "The people lie upon the ground, upon the breast of the All Mother, to give thanks to the All Father who sleeps within her. It is done to pray for guidance, for fertility, for success in hunting, and for the All Father's blessings. The Ritual of Prayer is meant for *prayer*. Fannon did not pray. His action was a mockery and in doing so he has blasphemed. To do as he suggests, to assume the position of the Ritual of Prayer in order to make contact with the people, is to suggest a course of blasphemy."

"In that humans would merely be going through the motions in order to attract the Shades, and not actually praying?" said Paul.

"Yes. The Ones Who Were cannot prevent the humans from doing this, but we have entreated with them not to make a mockery of that which is to us most holy."

"You see, Paul," Nils said, "we can't use the Ritual of Prayer as a means of contact without causing pain to the Ones Who Were. Their faith is a matter of great importance to them. We don't want to offend or hurt them in any way."

"So we don't follow up on the only lead we've got," said Fannon bitterly. "At this rate, we're never going to make contact."

Paul nodded. "I understand." It was ironic. He was light-years away from Earth, yet here it was again, religion standing in the way of knowledge. Still, there was a possible way around it.

"K'itar," he said, "from your merging with Shelby, are you aware that many humans are plagued with doubts concerning the existence of God, what you call the All Father?"

"It is a sad thing," said K'itar.

"Be that as it may," said Paul, "it is in human nature to doubt. Even the most pious, holy humans have doubted in the past. I myself was raised a Christian. It is a Christian belief that God, the All Father, gave us His only son so that He could suffer our sins."

"The one you call Jesus," K'itar said.

"Yes. And history, Christian history, at any rate, tells us that even Jesus doubted at one time. Perhaps that was how the Creator made us. If we did not doubt, then we would not have the urge to *know*. And without that urge, humanity would never have embarked upon the course that brought us here. I'll tell you honestly, K'itar, that I doubt God exists. I doubt that the All Father exists."

"Paul . . ." said Nils. Paul responded by placing a hand on Björnsen's forearm, reassuring him.

"I doubt that if the All Father exists, he is both God *and* the All Father, the same Supreme Being or even different facets of that Being. I *doubt* that, but I'm not saying that it's so. You see, I don't know for sure. I don't deny, I doubt."

K'itar/Shelby nodded, slowly.

I would like to believe that God exists," said Paul. "I would like to believe that our God and your All Father are the same, that He is *here*. I think that would be wonderful. But I am what I am, as is Fannon, as is Nils, as are all the rest of us. We may not have your faith, but would it still be blasphemy if we were to perform the Ritual of Prayer to ask forgiveness for having unwittingly made a mockery of it, to do so sincerely, even while our doubt remains? And would it be blasphemy if, for example, Fannon were to perform the Ritual of Prayer the next time he met one of your people in order to pray that our two races might find a way to come together? To do so even while his doubt remained? Because I don't think Fannon can rid himself of doubt. I don't think any human can. That, too, is doubt. It's the way we are, the way we were created, by whoever or whatever was responsible."

There was a long silence.

"Your doubt will not change what is," K'itar said at last. "If you were to pray sincerely, then it would not be blasphemy."

"I think I'd like to go and lie down for a while," Shelby said. "I'm getting a headache."

She got up and left the mess hall. Paul sighed. There was a long, tense moment of silence during which no one spoke. No one. Paul realized that everyone in the mess hall had gathered around their table. They were surrounded by a crowd.

"I'm beginning to see why they sent you," Fannon said. "You finessed your way through that one pretty well. And it's only your first day here."

Paul stared at him and pursed his lips thoughtfully. He took a deep breath.

"I'm not so sure that 'finesse' is the right word," he said. "I

34

really had no idea of what I was doing at all. Your implication is that I subtly manipulated the Ones Who Were into seeing things your way." He shrugged. "Perhaps there was some manipulation involved. I have a feeling that if I think about it very much, I'll only get confused. I was in error, though. In my approach. Shelby does not have a split personality. From everything I've learned about the Shades, it would seem that she has the potential for a personality much more fully integrated than any of ours. I would like to spend a great deal more time with her. I can't imagine what it must be like. To this K'itar entity, the existence of a Supreme Being is not just a matter of belief. The Shades accept it as a fact. *We* may have some doubts on that account, and the human part of Shelby Michaels is no different from us in that respect. Only how does she reconcile that with her nonhuman aspects? How is it possible to accept something as an irrevocable truth and yet doubt it at the same time?"

Fannon looked away, uneasily.

"And then you might consider another possibility," said Paul. "Mind you, I doubt it very much, but suppose K'itar is right?"

# CHAPTER FOUR

The *Blessing* was destroyed. M'uri did not know it was the *Blessing*; she did not know it was a ship. If someone had told her that it was an FTL ship, she would not have known what that was, either. She only knew that there had been a great flash in the night sky unlike anything she had ever seen before.

She would not have understood that an FTL ship's nuclear drive had been triggered to explode within a week, Earth relative time, of the opening of the five thousand cryogens aboard. She would not have understood that the ship had been destroyed so that a human survey team that would not come for another thousand years would find no evidence of it. She knew only that there had been a fire in the sky and that *they* had come.

She had never seen anything like *them* before. They were not beasts, surely, for they did not look like beasts. They looked almost like the people, but they were not of the people. Their skin was a peculiar color, like that of the inside of a fish. Their manes were strange, some dark, some light, all different shades, and some had no manes at all. Their eyes were not like the eyes of the people. They, too, were colored differently, and they looked lifeless. They did not glow. It did not seem to M'uri that they could see well. They were smaller than the people, thicker, and their hands had too many fingers, but most of all—and this she found the most astonishing—she could not sense that they had ever *been* before. They had no Ones Who Were! Surely, then, these were not people. But if they were not beasts, and if they were not people, then what *were* they?

They all grouped together, something the people did not do, except during the time of Need, the time of mating. She thought when she first saw them that it was a time of Need for them, but she did not understand their Rituals if that was so. They did not dance; there was no choosing. Instead, they all stayed together, working, yet performing work that made no sense to her. Taking care of their domain, that would have been something she could have understood. Healing trees that were not well, rerouting streams, that would have made sense, but what they did was all a mystery to her. They had . . . things, things she had never seen before, and with these things they made even larger things, things much larger than themselves. They damaged their domain terribly, razing all growing things to make an area of land that was bare, a sight that was almost as frightening as the burned-out ground in the center of which sat some giant beast that did not move, a beast that somehow reflected light. She had seen them entering this beast and then coming out of it again. What strange creature was this? The things they made were like this creature. Perhaps it was not a creature, but a thing. But what *kind* of thing?

"They are cursed creatures," said her Great Father, R'nal. "They bare the breast of the All Mother and make large, unholy things."

"But where have they come from?" said M'uri, feeling frightened.

"I do not know," said Great Father R'nal. "But they are on our domain."

"They have not sought out the One That Is to challenge," M'uri said.

"They are some new kind of beast," D'ali, the Father Who Walked in Shadow, said. "Beasts do not challenge for domain. But there are too many to bring down at once."

"We must pray to the All Father," said Great Mother N'tani. "We must ask for guidance."

M'uri had prayed, but an answer did not come. Perhaps she had not prayed hard enough. Perhaps she had somehow proved herself unworthy and could not hear the All Father's reply. Things were not clear, and even her Ones Who Were did not know what to do. This frightened M'uri very much.

"We've spotted one," said James.

Wendy felt a strange surge of exhilaration. "Where?"

"Just beyond the perimeter, on the far side of the shuttle," James said. "It's a female. I don't think she knows we've seen her."

"Excellent," said Wendy. "Pull everybody back, away from the shuttle. Get out of sight. Try to get it done quietly, so as not to scare her off. Let's see if we can't get her inside the perimeter. Shut the field down on the shuttle side of the base."

With everyone else out of sight, Wendy hid behind a partially erected dormer and watched. It took a long time, but finally the Shade began to move forward, hesitantly, cautiously. It was fascinated by the shuttle. It approached slowly, holding its spear extended, as if expecting attack.

Just a little more, thought Wendy, barely able to contain her excitement. Just a little farther . . .

She was inside the perimeter! Wendy activated the Sturmann field.

"Okay," said Wendy into her communicator, "we've *got* her!

They moved in on the Shade. Her first reaction was to flee, but she got only as far as the perimeter. Running full-speed, the Shade came into contact with the field. There was a sputtering, popping sound and the Shade was hurled back several yards. She fell, stunned, and her wooden catapult dropped out of her hand. Wendy held her rifle ready. The Shade moved sluggishly upon the ground, fumbling for her spear. Wendy leveled her rifle and fired a stun charge. The Shade went limp.

The Shade struggled against the restraints, but they were secure. Wendy could feel the empathic projection of her fear. It was a lucky thing the ability was only latent in the Shades. If it was a force they could control, it could make a handy weapon, but Wendy knew it for what it was and did not allow it to affect her.

"Hold her," Wendy said. "Be careful! I don't want the knife to slip. If she dies right away, we'll lose her."

Two men held the thrashing Shade still while a third approached her with a knife. The cuts were made carefully, lengthwise and very deep. The blood began to flow freely from the Shade's wrists.

"All right, now back away," said Wendy. "Let her realize that no Shade will answer her Call before she dies."

It did not take long. The blood gushed from M'uri's wrists in arterial spurts. She had stopped struggling. It would be all over within a few minutes. The restraining straps upon the shuttle flight chair were soaked with blood. M'uri's eyes began to lose their bright glow as life ebbed from her veins. As Wendy watched, M'uri grew weaker and weaker. Then her hand fluttered like a wounded butterfly. Fighting against the restraints, M'uri reached out for her. Wendy quickly approached and allowed the Shade to Touch her.

It hurt more than she could have imagined. It felt as though a hot knife had been plunged into her brain. Involuntarily, she tried to jerk away, but found that she couldn't. For an instant, it was as though she had been welded to the Shade, then the contact was broken and she was hurled to the floor, toppled by her own efforts to break free. She was in agony. Her mouth opened in a long, soundless scream as she rolled around upon the shuttle floor, her hands clutching at her head. The mind sought retreat into shock from the pain, but it was no longer the same mind, it no longer worked the same way.

Countless images and memories churned within her, flashing in and out of her consciousness with blurring intensity, nothing she could identify, nothing she could hold on to. Her eyes rolled up in their sockets from the sheer overload of input, from the invasion into the innermost recesses of her being by countless alien identities, from the *pain*, the pain that was unlike any she had ever known before.

The Shade was dead, its body slumped in the chair, its thick white mane obscuring its face.

She was aware of hands upon her, of her fellow Seedlings trying to help her up. It wasn't happening to her. It was happening to someone else. She was aware of struggling against them, though she had not thought to struggle. It was as though someone else were doing the struggling, she was just observing, trapped helpless within her own body, a passive entity, a puppet with its strings being awkwardly manipulated by alien puppeteers.

They held her tightly, trying to prevent her uncoordinated flailing. The dead Shade was taken out of the chair and dumped upon the floor. She was put in its place, slammed down onto the flight chair that was slick with Shade blood, held down, strapped in. They crowded all around her, as many as could fit inside the shuttle, watching anxiously.

Her struggles ceased. She became aware of going limp. She tried to will herself to move, to make some little motion, to raise a finger, and found that she could not. She had no control. The memory of the searing pain caused by the merging was still fresh, but she no longer really felt it. Instead, there was a growing numbness, a sense of drowsiness, an almost ethereal withdrawal from her body. She didn't want to fight it, but she was conditioned to, and she struggled with the feeling. However, the initial contact had left her weak and overwhelmed with pain. Gradually, she lost the struggle and slipped into a dream.

Even in the dream, she fought them. The Ones Who Were, creatures of pure psychic energy, plunged deep into her mind, rifling through her personality like an ancient computer sorting punch cards. With the speed of thought, they hurtled through her conscious mind, skirting the edges of her subconscious, as though afraid to venture there. There were too many images, too many memories flooding into her, generations upon generations of experience that threatened to overwhelm her sanity. As had happened once before, when she had first come to Boomerang with the original survey team, she was subjected to an awesome assault. It had happened long ago. Since then, she had been cured, had been conditioned, but now it all came back to her and she was unable to repress the memory of an incident that would not happen for another thousand years.

M'uri was terrified. When she had realized what the strange new creatures intended to do, she had fearfully looked to the Ones Who Were for guidance, but they had not been able to help her. They despaired, because they too realized that the alien beings intended for them to die, truly die, without being able to merge. How was it possible that any being could be so cruel? Even the hellhounds, nothing more than beasts, killed for a reason. They killed for survival, but these new beings seemed to want to kill just so that they could watch the death. The Ones Who Were could sense their anticipation. And then they sensed something else as well, something which terrified them even more. The strange new beings *were* killing for a reason. *They desired to merge.*

It was unheard of. Never had one Shade attempted to take, by force, the generations of another. Never had one Shade tried to kill another of its kind. When they challenged for domain, the Ritual was meant just to establish which was stronger. That was the Way, the weak always gave way before the strong, it was unnecessary to kill, it was unthinkable. Yet it became clear to M'uri's Ones Who Were that the aliens were doing precisely that, killing the One That Is in order to force M'uri to merge with them. There was no choice. Either M'uri bestowed the Touch upon one of the alien beings, or an entire tribe would experience the true death. As life ebbed from M'uri's veins, she reached out to one of the aliens in desperation.

The alien allowed the Touch, came forward eagerly to bear it, and M'uri, the One That Is, became one of the Ones Who Were as they left their body and merged with that of the alien who had never *been* before.

Frightened, M'uri clung to her Great Father, R'nal, as they merged with the alien. They had to live, they *had* to survive, but R'nal did not know if they could do so within this strange new being called a *human*. R'nal did not know if this Wendy human meant to somehow consume them, to absorb their energy and feed on them in some way, so R'nal guided the Ones Who Were on a dizzying journey through the Wendy entity, fearing to linger for too long in any facet of her mind lest they should somehow be absorbed. M'uri had never known R'nal to be frightened before. She was a small thing in their gestalt, not yet integrated into the Ones Who Were. She . . . and they . . . were lost.

As they plumbed the depths of the human's mind, trying to find a way to coexist with Wendy, they encountered numerous memories, images, and sense impressions the like of which they had never known before.

These humans had come from the stars, come to the All Mother on that great light in the sky. The humans had no Ones Who Were, but their number was legion. They had achieved great things. They could fly through the sky and live in the empty blackness of the night. R'nal saw human cities, he saw human colonies spread out throughout the universe. The humans were more powerful than any other creature that existed, and R'nal and all the Ones Who Were felt small and insignificant.

*The humans came from the All Father.*

As Wendy struggled in her dream that was not quite a dream, a memory that had been repressed began to surface, as it had been meant to do. It had happened long ago; it would not happen for another thousand years. She sought not to confront it, but the confrontation was inevitable. Wendy remembered.

*She lay sprawled upon the forest floor, tears making tracks in the dirt that caked her face, fingers clutching at the earth. She whimpered like a child and lowered her head onto a section of gnarled root at the base of a large tree that draped its large fronds over her. She had been running aimlessly through the forest, oblivious of the branches that lashed her face, lacerating her about the cheeks and eyes. She was bruised and battered from her flight and drenched with sweat. She was physically exhausted, but she felt no pain. No physical pain. It seemed to her that she was isolated, lost inside her head, divorced not only from her body, but from her surroundings, too.*

*Hours before, there had been some vague homing instinct that had driven her toward the ship's lighter, toward the closest thing to home that existed for her on an alien world. But that homing instinct was long gone. It had been driven out by panic and hysteria until all that remained was an animal urge to flee, to somehow find someone or something she could hold on to, something familiar, some reassurance that the fragile fabric of her reality had not been torn to shreds. There was a maelstrom in her mind that would not subside. She tried with all her will to fight it, but she broke.*

*The defeated creature that huddled on the ground bore scant resemblance to Lieutenant Win T'ao Chan, a resilient and highly trained specialist, an officer in Colonization Command. The last thing that Lieutenant Chan had seen had been a pair of shockingly violet eyes that seemed to burn with an opalescent fire. The image still lingered.*

*She had been examining a blighted tree. Kneeling on the ground, she could see that some sort of balm had been applied to the tree at its base, a mixture of mud and what appeared to be pulped compost composed of leaves and berry fruit and tiny rootlets. It was clear evidence of the Shades' in-*

41

*timate involvement with their domains. The earth at the base of the tree had been dug up, the roots had been exposed, the same mixture applied directly to the roots and piled around them, and then the roots had been covered with earth once more. She was taking samples when she became aware of no longer being alone. She looked up, expecting to see Drew Fannon or Nils Björnsen, but it was a Shade. She caught her breath and did not move, for fear of frightening the being.*

*It stood just out of reach, staring at her curiously. She felt its sadness. A deep sense of melancholy began to fill her being, a melancholy that rapidly grew to profound depression and then to abject despair. She saw herself, suddenly, as the Shade saw her, a being hopelessly alone, entombed within her own ego. She had no Great Father, upon whose wisdom she could rely for guidance. She had no Great Mother, whose love and stabilizing influence could support her. She had no Great Hunter, who could protect her and guide her own development as a survivor. She had no Father Who Walked in Shadow, who kept her in touch with but separate from her darker, animal nature, who was her most basic link to her primordial past. And she had no Healer, who could protect her from the distress she was now feeling. She was a human, she had no Ones Who Were, she could not Touch and merge, she would not continue. She would live her life alone, as she had always lived it, never knowing the true intimacy of spiritual contact, never knowing the blessings of the All Father. And she would die the true death, die as she had lived, alone. She felt the Shade's pity for her, and she staggered to her feet, holding out her arms as if to keep the empathic projection of the Shade at bay. She could feel it better, more profoundly, than any of the others because of the latent esper potential that she had been born with, the ability she had tried to repress since her early childhood because too often it had given her glimpses into the souls of others, knowledge she had never asked for, perceptions that had hurt.*

*She had cried out and fled, running from the Shade, running from herself, unable to deal with experiencing herself as an unutterably lonely being, cut off from everything that mattered. She ran, sobbing, through the forest, tripping over roots and vines, falling, getting up again, feeling no pain, feeling nothing but the most profound despair she had ever known.*

She did not remember what happened after that. She did not remember how Fannon and Björnsen had finally found her, withdrawn into catatonia, how they had placed her into a cryogen and revived Shelby Michaels to take her place on the mission team while she stayed in coldsleep until such time as they could get her proper care. She did not remember how she had returned from Boomerang. She had only vague memories of being treated at a ColCom base, of everything that had happened to her up until the time that she revived from coldsleep aboard the *Blessing*. Fannon and Björnsen would not arrive on Boomerang for another thousand years. When they came, *she* would come with them. Only she was already here. She had failed before; now the All Father had given her another chance.

"And we will help you," said R'nal, within her mind.

"You will help me?" she said in her dream, and, in the waking world, her fellow Seedlings who crowded around her saw her lips move, but no sound came forth and they could not tell what she said.

"We are now a part of you," R'nal said. "We know what you know. You are the One That Is now. There is much that we have yet to learn, much that we have yet to understand, but it was the will of the All Father that this should be so."

"Yes, the will of the All Father. You must become like us. We must become like you. That is why we were sent."

"It will take time," R'nal said. "This is a different merging than that which we know. It frightens you. It frightens us. Yet we will survive. The All Father has acted in His wisdom to bring this thing about. We will not fail Him. Rest now. S'utar will ease your troubles. We have much to do."

Wendy felt the soothing presence of the Healer, S'utar, as the entity became dominant in her conscious mind. Again, she involuntarily attempted to resist the Healer's influence, to retain her dominance, but she was totally exhausted and could not resist with all her will. Still, the Ones Who Were marveled at her strength and sense of purpose. And, as Wendy slept, watched over by her fellow Seedlings, the Ones Who Were became divided in their tasks. M'uri still clung to the Great Father. She was not yet fully integrated into the gestalt, but there would be time for that. There was still much to learn about the One That Is, the first human they had ever known.

As the Healer gently eased Wendy into restful sleep, Great Mother N'tani took control, guiding Wendy's dreams, teaching her about the Shades, about the Rituals and the Way. R'nal, along with D'ali, the Shadow aspect, sought to plumb the depths of Wendy's psyche, to know and understand her thoroughly so that they could all coexist. There was an area

43

within Wendy's subconscious that resisted all their probings and D'ali sought to break through the barriers, but his actions agitated Wendy and N'tani was afraid that she would lose control, so they decided to explore that area more fully at another time. They had a lot of time now.

While Wendy slept, her dreams guided by N'tani, her mind gently investigated by R'nal and D'ali, her pain and discomfort eased by S'utar, T'ral kept watch. The Seedlings clustered around Wendy saw her open her eyes and look at them, but it was a feral look, the gaze of a wild beast. The gaze of the Great Hunter.

"She sleeps," he said to them through Wendy's lips, using their own language.

They seemed to understand. They gestured to each other and they left the shuttle, leaving the One That Is alone. The door slid shut, but T'ral could sense them keeping guard outside. Slowly, gently, while the One That Is slept, T'ral rose from the chair, testing the body. If there was need to fight in order to protect the One That Is, T'ral had to be ready.

James heard Wendy moving about inside the shuttle. He sighed. He did not go in.

# CHAPTER FIVE

Fannon closed the door behind him and sat down on the small sofa, stretching out his muscular frame. He shook some dark hair out of his eyes with a quick toss of his head and accepted the coffee Paul offered him. The office they were in was spartan. It was small and contained only the sofa, several comfortable chairs, a low table, and a utilitarian desk upon which sat a small computer terminal.

"Am I your first?" said Fannon.

"First what?"

"Patient, case, whatever."

Paul smiled, "You're the first one I've asked to speak to,

44

besides Jake on the trip out. I'd like to get around to everyone eventually, but I have no intention of thinking of anyone as being a 'case' or a 'patient' unless they come to me to seek out my services in that regard. Why, do you feel like a patient?"

"No," said Fannon. "What did you want to talk about?"

"Oh, various things," Paul said with a shrug. "Yourself, the mission, how you feel about it and the people you're working with, the Shades . . ."

"Shelby," said Fannon.

"Yes, I especially wanted to talk about Shelby," Paul said.

"I figured you would. Can we talk about you, too?"

"If you like."

"Okay. Shoot."

"Why are you here?" said Fannon.

"Because the Directorate—"

"That's not what I meant," said Fannon. "I mean, what were your reasons for leaving a cushy job with SEPAP to take an unknown assignment in the field?"

"I see you've already discussed me with Jake," said Paul.

"Some. But I want to hear it from you."

"Very well. It was, as you said, a 'cushy job.' However, it simply wasn't enough. It wasn't money, I had plenty of that. It was opportunity. I had none of that at all. I wanted a challenge. I wanted a change. I wanted to work with people once again. I wanted to do something that would make me feel young or, at least, younger. I was tired of the grind, of doing the same thing every day, of not having my mettle really tested, as it were. So . . . He shrugged and spread his hands out. "When the Directorate requested that I undertake this assignment, I jumped at the chance."

"Just like that?" said Fannon. "Without knowing anything about it?"

"Well, I *did* know that it was important, else they would not have asked me. It obviously involved a challenge. It involved a top-secret mission, which made it sound quite fascinating, and it involved a rather radical change in life-style and routine, which was exactly what I had been looking for, although to be quite truthful, I hadn't known it until the opportunity came along. The thought occurred to me in passing that it might be dangerous, but even that seemed exciting. Besides, how dangerous could it be? I would be surrounded by highly trained field personnel. I didn't exactly go into it completely blind."

Fannon pursed his lips thoughtfully. "I don't know, Doc. It's a little hard to buy."

"Why? How much did you know about what you were getting into when you were active as a sleeper survey officer? Considerably less than I knew, I should think. Don't you believe that someone in my position could be just as susceptible to the lure of adventure as yourself?"

"I don't know. Maybe," Fannon said. He grinned. "Adventure was what got me into it, but that was a long, long time ago. You weren't even born then."

"You say it was what got you into it. Past tense?"

"You mean what kept me going?" Fannon said. "Sometimes I'm not entirely sure. Sometimes I think it was just inertia."

"Now I find *that* a little hard to buy," said Paul. "Even if that were the case, I should think the Rhiannon mission would have taken care of that."

Fannon glanced at him sharply. "I don't know why I'm surprised," he said. "I should have known you'd do your homework."

"I have complete files on all the mission personnel," said Paul. "Yours is more interesting than most."

"Yeah, well, if you've seen the file, then you'll know what happened on Rhiannon and how I felt about it. As I recall, I made my feelings abundantly clear at the debriefing sessions."

"Indeed you did," said Paul. "And I empathize."

"You do, huh?"

"Rhiannon was long before my time," said Paul. "I have never labored under the illusion that ColCom's interests were anything more than self-serving, but I was still upset to learn that genocide of an entire race was actively considered as an option to make Rhiannon viable for colonization."

"Only upset?" said Fannon. "I was *outraged*. I was . . . there aren't even words to say how I felt. Sure, the natives of Rhiannon were hostile, but they were *sentient*, for God's sake!"

"Does that make the idea more abhorrent?" said Paul.

"Doesn't it to you?"

"Well, let's say that if they weren't sentient, it would not have made it any less abhorrent to me. But history is chock full of cases where precisely that sort of hair-splitting made the difference. Consider the Amerind. One of the most effective ways of preparing yourself to deal with an enemy—and in this case, by enemy I mean someone who has something that you want or stands in the way of your achieving something—has been to dehumanize that enemy. To make it all right to do away with him because he's something less than you are. He's a savage, a barbarian, an animal, an embodiment of evil. Considering that such logic was practiced throughout human history, is it then surprising that it be applied to beings who are *demonstrably* inhuman?"

"What are you trying to say? That it was all right just because the Rhiannans were aliens?" said Fannon.

"No, I'm not exercising a value judgment here, just trying to put things in perspective. You, more than anyone else, with the exception of the people who were with you on that mission, were in a better position to accept that sort of logic, because you had direct evidence of the Rhiannans inhumanity, of their savagery, their hostility. They tried to kill you."

"So I should have hated them for that and said, yes, go ahead, wipe them out, it's okay with me?"

"It certainly would not have been an abnormal reaction. It would have made even more sense that someone who was kept in the service by, as you say, inertia, would have experienced that event as a breaking point and left. Yet you stayed. Why?"

Fannon was silent for a moment before answering.

"I thought of quitting then," he said. "I didn't want to ever go through anything like that again. But I just couldn't. I couldn't let something like that drive me out. It would look as if I left because I couldn't take it, because I was afraid."

Paul nodded.

"I told myself then, just one more mission. Just one more, to prove to myself, if to no one else, that I wasn't scared. That I *could* take it. Just one more, so I wouldn't be leaving with a bad taste in my mouth."

"And?"

Fannon shrugged. "Well, as you can see, I'm still here. I went on that next mission, then said just one more. And just one more after that. And one more after that. And then I just stopped counting."

"So there would seem to be more involved than just proving something to yourself, because I would say that you had done that amply," Paul said.

"Well, someone's got to do it."

"True, but why you?"

"Maybe because I care that it gets done right," said Fannon. "ColCom doesn't care. They never did. They would have wiped out the Rhiannans if they hadn't become con-

47

vinced that it wasn't cost-effective. They may make the final decisions, but there has to be someone in the field who makes the right decisions first. Someone's got to be responsible."

"Do you feel responsible for the Shades?" said Paul.

"Ah, now we're getting to it," Fannon said. "Yes, I feel responsible. This planet is a first-class piece of real estate. It wouldn't take much to establish a human colony world here. *But*, a human colony would not be able to coexist with the Shades. The balance would be far too fragile. A human colony would disrupt the ecosystem, of which the Shades are a vital part. It would disrupt the Shades' structure of domain, interfere with their territorial imperative, their entire method of living. I think a human colony would have destroyed the Shades. Utterly. We would have rolled right over them. ColCom had to have a damn good reason not to do that."

"And you gave them one?"

"Turns out I gave them a hell of a good reason, although I hadn't meant to," Fannon said. "At least, not in the way that it turned out."

"How's that?" said Paul.

"I had no way of knowing about the plague drug and its effects," said Fannon. "All that happened while we were out here, Nils, Wendy, and myself. And Shelby."

"By Wendy you mean Lieutenant Chan, the one whom Shelby replaced?" said Paul.

Fannon nodded. "We could have gone back then," he said. "Without ever having revived Shelby to involve her in the fieldwork itself. We could have gone back *before* Wendy became a casualty. We had enough data to enable us to conclude that the Shades were sentient, but I wanted to have all our questions answered, I wanted to be able to present a really strong case to ColCom."

"It sounds to me as though you're accepting the responsibility for a lot of things that happened on that mission that you had no control over," Paul said.

"Wendy's becoming catatonic, you mean?" said Fannon. "Yeah, well, I've raked myself over the coals about that pretty thoroughly. Maybe it wasn't really my fault. I never thought that she was cut out for fieldwork. She wasn't really strong enough. But there's no denying that it would not have happened if I hadn't been so hardnosed about getting all the data straight."

"Because you didn't trust ColCom to make the right decision?" Paul said.

"Yeah," said Fannon. "At that point, with what we had, it

could have gone either way. They could easily have disagreed with our conclusions and classified the Shades as animals, which would have made it perfectly acceptable to push them out of the way."

"From what I gather of your impressions about their behavior during the Rhiannon affair, they could easily have done that anyway," said Paul, "regardless of how well you had done your job, of how strong a case for sentience you presented."

"That's true," said Fannon. "If they had, I would have fought them to the extent that I was able. It might not have done much good. They stuck me out here, and there doesn't seem to be anything that I can do about it. But at least I'd have the knowledge that *I* had done the right thing. I'm not sure how much consolation that would have been, but it would have been something."

"You don't like ColCom very much, do you?" Paul said.

Fannon snorted. "Whatever gave you that idea?"

"What about Shelby?" Paul said.

"What about her?"

"How do you feel about what's happened to her? Do you feel any responsibility for that?"

"I *am* responsible," said Fannon. "She was our pilot. She should never have been part of the survey team itself. When Wendy broke down, I was the one who talked Nils into reviving Shelby to take her place. Neither of us was especially thrilled with the idea, but I think Nils resisted it more than I did."

"So if you hadn't revived Shelby, she would never have experienced her transformation."

Fannon nodded.

"Do you have any feelings of guilt about what happened?"

"This is getting to be quite some talk," said Fannon.

"We could stop, if you like."

"No. It's all right. You're just trying to do your job, right? We want to make sure that the Directors get a complete report, don't we?"

"I consider anything said in this room privileged communication," Paul said. "Or is it that you don't trust me?"

"I didn't say that. But you *are* ColCom."

"As are you, if you choose to look at it that way. I'm also a psychiatrist."

"And I'm not your patient. Isn't that what you said?"

49

"Yes, of course. Is it that you perceive me to be one of 'them'? A stooge of the Directorate or what?"

"There is the fact that you'll be making those flights back with Jake to report to them," said Fanon.

"That changes nothing," Paul said. "My first responsibility is still to the people here, just as you see your first responsibility as being to make the right decisions, rather than the ones that might be more convenient for ColCom."

"I see your point," said Fannon. "Look, don't get me wrong, Paul. I'm not a paranoid. But you were handpicked by the Directors. I've met the Directors. I've met Directors past and present and I don't like them."

"Do you feel threatened by them?"

Fannon laughed. "Hell, they *exiled* me here! Took the results of the Boomerang survey and everyone even remotely connected with it and tucked it all away neatly under file and forget. Except they haven't quite forgotten it, have they? Jake has standing orders to report to them every time he makes a supply run, and suddenly you show up, SEPAP personnel, talking about how a person with your expertise was needed on this mission and making noises about ColCom's being concerned about the psychological welfare of the people on Boomerang. That doesn't sound a lot like the ColCom I know. They *want* something. I don't know what it is yet, and that makes me suspicious. So you can enter into your desk terminal that Captain Drew Fannon is exhibiting paranoid tendencies or whatever; frankly, I don't care."

"You feel a lot of anger, don't you?" Paul said.

"Yeah. So what does that make me?"

Paul shrugged elaborately. "I don't know. An angry man?"

Fannon chuckled. "All right, so I'm being a bit edgy, a bit defensive. I'll lighten up."

"Can we get back to Shelby?"

"All right."

"We were talking about responsibility and guilt," said Paul.

"Yeah. Responsibility. Yes, I feel responsible. Guilt? Yeah, that too."

"You don't think she might be better off as she is now?" said Paul. "Consider what she was before. A sleeper pilot. A profound neurotic who lived out her waking life aboard a ship, in self-imposed isolation, unable to bear human society—"

"Yes, I know," said Fannon, "but that was the way she was. And what she did with her life was her *choice*. From the

50

moment we revived her from coldsleep and made her part of the team, she had no choices."

"And what about now?" said Paul.

"Does she have any choices now?" Fannon sighed. "I honestly don't know."

"Why don't you know?" said Paul.

"The human Shelby Michaels is a part of something that's much larger now," said Fannon. "There's Shelby, and then there are the Ones Who Were. She's a part of them and they're a part of her, but I can't help feeling that she's somehow outnumbered."

"She's much more than just a friend to you, isn't she?" Paul said.

"That's no secret," Fannon said.

"How do you relate to her?"

"I'm not sure I understand," said Fannon.

"Well, judging by my own reactions," Paul said, "and I've hardly spent any time with her at all, I should think that it would be very hard to become accustomed to the fact that there is really no such thing as a one-to-one relationship with Shelby. Conversationally, it's easy to address her in the singular. It's hard to keep in mind that you are actually addressing a vast number of personalities simultaneously when just one body is seated before you, but the fact of the matter is that Shelby is eternally in the plural, isn't she? Or rather, aren't they? It's awkward for me to even talk about it. How must it be for you?"

"Scientific curiosity, Doctor?" Fannon said.

Paul nodded. "Partly. I'd be a liar if I didn't admit to that. But I'm also trying to understand her, which is a large part of why I wanted to see you first."

"Understanding her ain't easy," Fannon said.

"Do you?"

"Understand her? More than anybody else, I guess. Except maybe Nils. It's easier to accept what she's become than to understand it. You've seen her, spoken with her. It isn't hard to get along with her; she makes it easy. The Ones Who Were are well aware of how important our own egos are to us. Shelby *acts* human most of the time; the Ones Who Were tend to stay in the background, to let her do a lot of the talking for them. Most of the people here are comfortable, thinking of her as being a human being with multiple personalities. That isn't so, as you yourself realized early on. Intellectually, we all understand that, but it's another thing to attempt to

51

deal with it on a gut, emotional level. She has no individuality, in any sense of the word, at least not the way we understand it. She's become a unique life form."

"Interesting that you should say that," Paul said. "I noticed when I first met her that she said something about how hers are not the perceptions of a human being."

"Well, that's the bottom line," said Fannon. "She isn't human."

"No, she isn't," Nils said softly. The evening breeze was ruffling his fine blond hair. "I'm not sure how many of us really realize that."

"What about her life before the merging?" Paul said. "She was human then. How has the merging changed that? She has gained alien personalities, but surely she's still human."

Nils nodded, twisting a stalk of flowering grass in his hands. "That's what we thought at first," he said. "That's how we felt. She's still Shelby, she still looks like Shelby—that was before her physical mutation—she's still got Shelby's personality. It's not as if her body had been taken over by the Shades, she was still there, *is* still there. Only we kept thinking in discrete terms. They don't apply. The Shelby Michaels that we knew before the merging no longer exists. Oh, in the strictest sense, she does, but she no longer matters as an individual."

"What about when I was speaking to her during dinner?" Paul said. "First I spoke to her, then I spoke with K'itar, the Great Father entity, then I spoke to her again. She said she had a headache and needed to lie down. Who had the headache? Shelby? K'itar? All of them?"

Nils smiled. "In point of fact, none of them."

"I don't understand."

"A headache would hardly incapacitate Shelby," Nils said. "She could very easily delegate the responsibility of feeling pain to one of her group entities, probably S'eri, the Healer. I am quite certain that what she was feeling was psychic distress of some sort and that it was necessary to excuse herself so that she could devote some time to reintegrating herself. Now, she didn't have to leave us in order to do that. She could have done that sitting right there, but then we would not have been exposed to Shelby."

"To whom would we have been exposed?" said Paul.

"T'lan, most likely. The Shadow is strongest at moments of psychic distress."

"Now you're starting to sound like a Jungian," said Paul.

"I've studied psychology," said Nils. "Amazing how many parallels there are, isn't it?"

"I find myself constantly debating the validity of applying human psychology to Shelby," Paul said. "I'm not certain that it wouldn't entail some risk."

"Well, Jung argued that archetypes were universal," Nils said with a smile. "What he wrote about the canalization of energy, for example, describing certain ceremonies among primitive peoples, can be applied directly to the Rituals of the Shades. If you're going to consider the group entities among the Ones Who Were as archetypes, then you can see their continuing process of integration as individuation in the Jungian sense, especially since it's an autonomous process."

"I had no idea you were a student of psychology," said Paul. "Your file gives no indication of it."

Nils grinned. "No, it wouldn't. That's because it's a recent avocation. And when Jake told me you had mentioned Jung, I boned up on him in the library."

"What did you think of my perception of the group entities as living archetypes?" said Paul.

"It fits," said Nils. "It also fits that they would serve as the transcendent function to unify the personality. That is what you meant when you said that Shelby has the potential to be much more fully integrated than any of us, isn't it?"

Paul nodded. He leaned back against the tree beneath which they sat and sighed.

"You feeling it?" said Nils.

"What?"

"A sort of sadness? A melancholia?"

Paul glanced at him quickly. "Is this *it*?" he said.

Nils nodded.

"It never would have occurred to me," said Paul with amazement. "It's so subtle! I thought it was all coming from me!"

"No, it's an empathic projection," said Nils. "There's a Shade out there somewhere, watching us." He stared out beyond the field. "We won't see him in this light unless we can spot the glow of his eyes."

"Is he close?" said Paul.

"I don't think so," Nils said. "It isn't very strong. It can be much stronger. Imagine what it would be like for an esper."

"You mean Wendy Chan."

Nils nodded. "It must have been unbearable. It caused her

to withdraw into herself completely. The Shades don't realize they do it, you know. At least Shelby's Ones Who Were didn't. Fannon calls them 'vibes.' It's all unconscious on their part. They feel sorry for us."

"Why?"

"Because we're all alone. We seem unutterably lonely to them. That's why they avoid us."

"You mean humans depress them?" said Paul.

"That's a good way of putting it," said Nils. "They also see us as being creatures of blasphemy. You've already had some indication of just how important their faith is to them. We have no Ones Who Were, so we've somehow been denied the blessings of the All Father. We denude the land, which they see as sacrilege. They don't quite know what to do about us. Every day, they draw back farther and farther from the base. Already, we're interfering with their structure of domain." He paused. "It's gone now. Do you feel it?"

"Yes."

"It takes a lot of getting used to." He changed the subject suddenly. "What did you make of Fannon?"

"Well, even though ours was not a doctor-patient discussion, I'm not sure I ought to say," said Paul.

"I'm worried about him," Nils said.

"Why?"

"We've been through a lot together. I've seen him in some pretty tough situations and he was always supremely in control. But he's been very edgy lately. He's a bundle of nerves, moody. He's under a great deal of strain."

"What do you think is causing it?"

"I know what's causing it," said Nils. "His relationship with Shelby." Nils shifted position on the ground and sat forward, shoulders slightly hunched. "Fannon's carrying a load of guilt around with him. He was involved with Wendy Chan. I don't know if you knew that."

"I didn't," said Paul. "I don't find it especially surprising, though. Intimate relationships are the norm for survey teams."

Nils nodded. "I had strong feelings for her too, but nothing like Fannon. He took it hard. He chose to blame himself for what happened. Part of him attempted to rationalize it by believing that Wendy was never cut out for survey work, that she lacked the temperament for it, that she was too fragile."

"Was she?"

"I don't believe so, no. It's possible, of course, but she did

54

make it through the training, and people who don't have what it takes for this sort of work are usually weeded out there. I think what happened was purely the result of her high degree of sensitivity to the Shades. That's not the same as being fragile. But Fannon has always felt that there should have been some way he could have prevented it."

"And Shelby?"

"Yes, that too," said Nils. "The thing is, his involvement with her didn't really begin until after the merging. Of course, she was much different before. You know how sleeper pilots are. They prefer their own company. Since the merging, she's changed a great deal, which is a hell of an understatement, come to think of it. You should have seen her before to truly appreciate the change, and I don't just mean the obvious one. She radiates a powerful charisma now. People are attracted to her. But for Fannon, it isn't quite the same. It's as you said, a one-to-one relationship with Shelby is impossible. It can't be easy to attempt to come to terms with the fact that your lover is a crowd. On an emotional level, I don't think Fannon really understands that. To be involved with Shelby means to be involved with K'itar and N'lia and S'eri, even T'lan, all of them."

"You think perhaps he resents having to share her with the Ones Who Were?" said Paul.

"I'm not sure what to think, Paul. You're the professional. You tell me."

"As a professional, I shouldn't tell you what to think," said Paul. "What does Shelby think?"

"Shelby understands," said Nils. "The Ones Who Were understand humans much better than we understand them, but then they have an advantage, don't they? There is a human element in their gestalt. If Fannon resents anything, I think it's their understanding."

"That's a quite insightful bit of observation for a layman," Paul said with a smile.

"Well, I know Fannon," said Nils. "I love him like a brother, but I wish to God he weren't here."

"Why?"

"Because it's all wrong for him. Everything. He's losing himself out here. There's a kind of man who really only functions at his best when he's at war. It doesn't mean that he loves war, that he loves killing, just that it gives him a sense of direction, of purpose. There was an old song lyric that went something like 'What do they do with a general when he stops being a general?' Fannon's whole life was being a survey officer. They've taken that away from him."

Paul frowned. "I wouldn't think so," he said. "What do you call all this?" He swept his arm out in an all-encompassing gesture, indicating the base and the world beyond it.

Nils smiled pensively. "It's not the same, though."

"How is it different?"

"Well, in a way, it's just too easy," Nils said. "Look around you. We have quite an installation here, all things considered. It's not the same as working out of a survey ship's lighter. There is still much to be done, a lot we have yet to learn here, but the challenge is nowhere near as great as coming to a planet cold, not knowing anything about it really, beyond the data picked up by a probe. Fannon's not in charge here. He doesn't even have a sense of being a real spacer anymore. He's landbound here. The technology has changed since the days we flew survey missions, and it's not Fannon against the world anymore."

"So you think perhaps he's channeling his frustrations inward and turning his energies against himself?" said Paul.

"Isn't that leading the witness, Doctor?"

"All right. What about Nils Björnsen?"

"Ah, well, Nils is a fatalist, you see. He never had any desire to be a general."

"What *does* he want?" said Paul.

Nils leaned back against the tree and stared off into the night. It was growing cold.

"When he was a little boy, young Björnsen dreamed of being a sailor," Nils said.

"He's landbound too now, isn't he?" said Paul softly.

Without looking at him, Nils nodded almost imperceptibly. For a long time, the two men just sat there in the cold night air, and neither spoke.

# CHAPTER SIX

The children were not allowed to venture out beyond the field. There was no disobedience. The temptation was there, of course, but two things prevented them from giving in to it. One was the field itself, which could teach a painful lesson in discipline; the other was the link each child had with its parents. There was no need to keep a close watch on the children in the Seedling colony. Each parent was aware, at all times, where the child was and what the child was doing.

The base had grown to twice its original size. Its perimeter was still guarded by the Sturmann poles, but now there was a mixture of the old and the new, of the modern and the primitive. They had constructed wooden cabins for each family with children, and new cabins were being erected all the time. Soon the village would be too large to be encompassed by the Sturmann field, but this had been part of the plan. By slow degrees, the Seedlings were going native.

All the Shades whose domains were in the vicinity of the village had been absorbed into the community. There were still many elders who had yet to become merged, and Drew was impatient for the day when all of them would have killed their own Shades. Then his turn would come. He would be the first, since he had been the first child born in the community.

He was eleven years old and already he was almost as tall as most of the elders. His hair was dark and hung down his shoulders, and his dark eyes were wild. He was the oldest and, as such, he was the leader of the other children, directing them in their games of Shade hunter and hellhound stalking. This time, Lani was the hellhound. She stood in the center of their circle, growling and snapping her teeth, making swiping motions with her hands, her fingers hooked like talons. The other children slowly closed the circle tighter.

Lani kept darting forward at them, then withdrawing. Drew hefted his spear in his right hand, then let it fly. It stabbed into the ground, missing Lani's bare right foot by a fraction of an inch. The other children took their cue from his action, and within seconds Lani was surrounded by a small grove of spears.

"Drew, that was too close!" she shouted.

"Did I cut you?" Drew said.

"No, but you *almost* did!"

"Then it was not too close."

"I don't want to be the hellhound anymore," she said. "I want to be a hunter!"

"When you learn to throw your spear well enough, then you can be a hunter," Drew said. He cut off her protests by raising his hand as he heard his mother's voice within his mind.

"Drew," said Wendy, "playtime is over. It's time to bring the children in for school."

He gathered them together and marched them to the training ground. His father, James, was waiting for them. They gathered around the shuttle, and when they had settled down, James led the prayer to the All Father. They all stretched out upon the ground, close to the All Mother's breast, and prayed for the All Father's blessings. They prayed that they would grow up to be strong, that they would all become good hunters, and that the task the All Father had set them would be met. When they were through, they all sat upon the ground and listened.

"Who are we?" James said.

"Seedlings!" they chorused.

"What are we?"

"Humans! Sent from the All Father!"

"Where do we come from?"

"From the stars!"

"Good," said James. "Today, we're going to talk about the Need. Does anyone know what the Need is?"

Drew raised his hand.

"Yes, Drew?"

"The Need is for bringing children into the world, to make the people strong," he said.

"Yes," said James, "that's part of it, but there is more. The Need is a feeling. It is a very strong desire. Shades experience the Need and it takes them over so that they can think of nothing else. They must travel to the place of mating high in the mountains and there they must take part in the Ritual of

Life. We are not like the Shades. We do not have a place of mating. Our Rituals are different. The Shades feel the Need at certain times, once in a great while, and it comes on all of them at once. We can feel the Need at any time, and it comes on us at different times. It is the way the All Father made us. The Shades can mate only once. After a mating has been successful and a child begins to grow, the Need is not felt again. We can mate many times and we always feel the Need. It does not go away."

Lani raised her hand.

"Does it hurt?" she said.

James smiled, "Sometimes it can hurt," he said, "but it does not hurt very much. Tonight, when you are home, ask your mother about what the Need is like for females. She will explain it to you. You are still too young for mating, but you should know about these things."

"Am I too young for mating?" Drew asked. "I am the oldest, so maybe I am ready?"

"You are almost ready," James said.

"How will I know when I am ready?"

"You will start to look at females differently," said James. "You will experience new feelings. I will explain all this to you, as all your parents will. The important thing for all of you to remember is that you must be strong. You must be healthy. And, above all, you must not give in to the Need until after you have killed your Shade and merged. This is our Way. You must all bear children, but for them to be blessed by the All Father, first you have to kill."

It was necessary for the hunting parties to go farther now. Sometimes they found a Shade close by, one who had been forced out of its domain by another Shade and had taken over the ground that had been claimed by one of those killed by the Seedlings. This did not happen often. The Seedlings found that they had to venture farther and farther from the village in order to capture Shades. Those who had merged had become better hunters as a result of the merging, for their Ones Who Were guided them in the task.

The All Father imposed many tests upon the people, and many of them could be cruel. The Ones Who Were who had merged with the Seedlings saw this test as the cruelest of them all, but it was the will of the All Father and, as the task was great, the test needed to be great as well.

It was hard for the Ones Who Were to accept that it was necessary to kill others of their kind, but it was the only way for them to merge with the Seedlings. When it had happened to them, they had felt great pain and had been frightened, but now they understood that the pain was part of it. The All Father had created humans and he had created the people. The humans, too, were people, but of a different kind. To each, the All Father had given different blessings. The humans were born lonely, denied Ones Who Were, but from their deprivation had come a different kind of unity. They had grouped together and had done great things. Still, Shades were more fortunate. The tests imposed upon them by the All Father were not nearly so great as those he had imposed upon the humans. They had had to prove themselves in the All Father's eyes before they could be brought to the All Mother, so that the two races could come together to create a third race, a combination of the two, a new creation of the All Father. Now that they had merged, these first beings of the new race had to carry on the task, to make others of their kind. And to do this, it was necessary that they kill. Out of death comes new life. This they had learned from the Seedlings.

There was still the specter of the true death to contend with. This was the great unknown. The newly merged Seedlings did not know if they could give the Touch. It was something humans could not do. It was for this reason that the All Father had brought them from the stars, so that they could learn. If the Ones Who Were who merged with them proved worthy, then perhaps the All Father would allow them to continue. Perhaps he would give his blessings to the Seedlings and give them the Touch. If they did not prove worthy, then the task would fall to the children. If it proved that the Seedlings could not merge, they might experience the true death. Then there would be only one chance for them to continue. If a live Shade were captured and placed with a dying Seedling, it would sense the presence of the Ones Who Were within that Seedling. It would know that they were dying. The Ones Who Were who had merged with the Seedlings knew from them that it was possible for a Shade to give the Touch and *take*. It was something that had not been done before in the memories of any of them. The Touch was always given by a dying One That Is. The Ones Who Were were *given* to another, not *taken* from another, yet the humans knew this could be done. There was no guarantee that a captured Shade placed in the presence of a dying Seedling would sense that Seedlings could not give the Touch, no way of knowing if that Shade would then attempt to *take* the Ones

Who Were, thereby preventing the true death. If that could be done, then the Shade who did the taking could be killed and forced to merge with one of the children. But the Shade might not know that it could or should take.

The Ones Who Were who had merged with Seedlings had come to look upon themselves as beings wholly different from the Shades. Superior. Closer to the All Father. This they perceived from the Seedlings. Within the minds of the humans were areas they could not explore. Hidden knowledge. The humans were strong, and they resisted when the Ones Who Were tried to penetrate into those areas. It caused them great distress. Perhaps, the Ones Who Were thought, if they proved worthy, they would be allowed access to this knowledge and they would learn the secrets placed there by the All Father. The human Ones That Are did not know these secrets, either. They were locked away from them as well. They became aware of them only when the Ones Who Were told them of these dark, hidden areas.

At night, the Seedlings would all gather in the meeting house after the children were asleep and they would talk for hours. This was an experience much appreciated by the Ones Who Were. They recalled a time, in their distant past, when there was speech among the Shades. As their number had grown greater over the years, they had become more self-contained. They had no great need to speak out loud, but it was good to listen to the Seedlings, to hear other Ones Who Were. There was still much they had to learn about these new beings from the All Father before they could truly transcend what they were and, like the Ones That Are, think of themselves as being human. They knew this was important. It was the will of the All Father.

Sometimes, late at night, Drew would awaken from strange dreams. He did not understand them. He felt them very strongly and he knew that they were wisdom from his mother, Wendy. He would sit up and look over at her lying down not far from him, see her open eyes questing all around as her Great Hunter, T'ral, kept watch while she slept. He would often speak with T'ral. He longed for a Great Hunter of his own.

T'ral did not understand this wisdom either. He would say, "She sleeps and dreams of secret knowledge." And that was all. His mother knew he shared her dreams, but she would never speak of them to him. The mornings after she had dreamed such dreams, she would grow quiet and disturbed. Drew never asked about them. He did not understand this secret knowledge, and it frightened him. Perhaps, when he was older, he would understand the visions.

They would come upon him suddenly, invading his own dreams, interrupting them and pushing them away. He would awake and sit there in the dark and still he would see the dreams as visions, because his mother slept and he received them from her. Sometimes the visions were so strong that even with his eyes wide open he could not see anything around him. Nothing but the visions.

He would see, as through his mother's eyes, a swirling mist of icy blue that grew thicker and enveloped him. He would grow very cold, even if the night was warm. It would seem to him that he could not move. There was something all around him, very close, containing him. There would be a window and he would be looking through it as he lay upon his back. He would hear a soft noise, a chiming unlike anything that he had heard before, and the window would move away, the mist would slowly dissipate. He would begin to move, slowly at first, feeling a stiffness in his joints and muscles. He would sit up.

He was in a ship. It was like the shuttle that they prayed around, only much, much larger. He would walk around inside it, hearing a gentle sound that he could not identify, not knowing where it came from. There would be lights and instruments and dials, like those inside the shuttle, only many more of them. And, like the shuttle, this ship would have windows. He would look out and see the stars.

# CHAPTER SEVEN

McEnroe slumped in his chair, one of his three priceless antique Dunhill pipes clamped between his teeth. "We've been at this for nine hours straight," he said wearily. "Let's quit for the day, I'm bushed."

"But we're getting close now," Shelby said.

"Look, you can put yourself on hold and catch forty winks while Big Daddy or whoever takes over," Sean said irritably. "*I* haven't got that luxury."

"Let's just run the last program one more time," she said.

"Oh, very well," said Sean. He leaned forward and punched it up. A series of semihuman sounds filled the room, raspy and guttural. They had been working from Shelby's voice speaking into a vodex harmonizer unit.

The harmonizer translated the audio signal, sampling the form and reducing it to a digital analog, assigning numbers to millionth-of-a-second sections of the wave. Coupled with a synthesizer capability, they had been working on a trial-and-error basis, eliminating possibilities, working with modulation and amplitude to lower and raise registers, eliminate and recombine sounds in an effort to produce the tones of the no longer spoken language of the Ones Who Were. Using a variable pitch capability, they had increased the speed without affecting the pitch and were, by slow degrees, coming closer to an approximation of the necessary sounds. However, it was still an approximation that they were approaching. They had yet to duplicate the real thing.

Shelby listened closely for a while and shook her head.

"It's still not right," she said. "We're getting there, but I just can't communicate the sounds to you. It's so exasperating! I can *hear* them in my head! If only you could hear my thoughts!"

"That's not the problem," Sean said. "What I need is an analog between *their* thoughts and yours."

"What do you mean?" she said.

"Well, it's simple, really. I could measure your brain waves with the EEG and translate it into acoustical speech, because I already have a model from which to work. It's simply a matter of assigning digital values and transposing . . ."

"What is it?"

"Let me talk to K'itar a minute, will you?" Sean said.

Shelby had grown accustomed to most of the base personnel treating the Ones Who Were as discrete entities. The fact that they were talking to all of the entities together when they spoke to her was irrelevant. It was easier for them to deal with the phenomenon of her merging as though they were all separate personalities within her mind, and it was easy for her to accommodate them. She allowed K'itar to speak through her directly.

"Yes, Sean?" K'itar said.

"K'itar, can you *hear* human speech the same way Shelby can hear yours?"

"I do not understand," the Great Father said.

"Shelby says that she can hear the language of the Shades in her mind. That she knows what it should sound like. Can you conceptualize human speech in the same way? In other words . . . damn, why didn't I think of this before? I think we just might have something here. Look. When the Ones Who Were communicate with the One That Is, with Shelby, how is that communication accomplished?"

"It is thought," K'itar said. "We know the thoughts of the One That Is and the One That Is knows our thoughts."

"Yes, yes," McEnroe said impatiently, "but how are those thoughts *framed?*"

K'itar hesitated a fraction of a second. "You are speaking of what humans call concepts?"

"Yes, yes, exactly."

"We share the knowledge of the One That Is," said K'itar. "There is nothing to correspond to our experience in the tools you use. We know what they are from the experience of the One That Is. We know her concept and understand it from her experience. In things that are familiar concepts to both Shades and humans, such as the hellhounds, which we call Rhann, although the sound we make now is not right—"

"Yes, hold it right there," McEnroe said eagerly, "That's precisely what I'm talking about. Areas of common conceptualization. Such as the hellhounds. Now, you can *say* the word in Shelby's mind, but you cannot make Shelby say the word correctly. Can you, in the same way, think of things the Shades and humans both have words for, think of them, that is, not with Shelby's mind, but with *yours?*"

"But . . . we are one," K'itar said. "We are the same."

"That's just it," McEnroe said excitedly, "you're not! You aren't discrete in that you are all linked together, like a series circuit, but what *are* you, K'itar? What are the Ones Who Were? You have no bodies, no corporeal form. You're psychic energy! And I think that can be measured! Thoughts are electrical impulses. You're so accustomed to being merged that you don't realize, or you never thought of it this way, that each Shade who once lived and still lives on in the Ones Who Were has psychic energy, an independence of a sort. You are all linked together, like the circuits in this computer, but it should be possible to break you down into your component forms, you see?"

"To . . . break down?"

"Don't worry, there's no danger. I have no intention of trying to find a way to disassemble the Ones Who Were. That's impossible, for all I know. What I was thinking of was to see if we could cause a temporary separation. It's like what I said before, the Shelby entity can grow tired and rest, while the other entities can carry on, employing the body or watching over it. True?"

"Yes."

"Right. Now . . . suppose Shelby, the One That Is, goes to sleep. She dreams, right?"

"That is correct."

"But you do not."

"No."

McEnroe licked his lips. "Shelby's EEG patterns would be different from that of an ordinary human. Because of you. Now, I could make a recording of Shelby's brain waves and program the computer to eliminate any patterns that would seem to deviate from the norm. We've got Shelby's files here, which means we have her medical records, so I've got access to an EEG recording of Shelby *before* she became merged. I could program that into the computer and, working from that and her present scan, we should be able to separate her brain-wave patterns from the thought impulses of the Ones Who Were."

"How does that help us create the sounds of the language of the people?" asked K'itar.

"It doesn't, yet," said McEnroe. "All that does is give me

an EEG reading on the Ones Who Were. It will still be a peculiar reading, I'm guessing, because the Ones Who Were are a gestalt. But we will have eliminated or separated Shelby's human brain waves. You know about coldsleep. There is a type of coldsleep wherein the brain is conditioned into a neutral alpha state, a dreamless, thought-free stasis. We know this can be done. Now, the question is, if Shelby can dream while the Ones Who Were remain conscious, and if the Ones Who Were can *guide* Shelby's dreams, is it not possible for the Ones Who Were to guide Shelby into a similar condition, a dreaming without dreaming, without thinking?"

K'itar hesitated only briefly. "S'eri and T'lan can do this. But what purpose would this serve?"

"It would give me a stronger signal on the thought patterns of the Ones Who Were," said McEnroe. "What we've got here is the basis for a fascinating experiment. Each human personality is, in essence, psychic energy. The Ones Who Were are no different in this respect. You coexist in Shelby's body, sharing the same nervous system. We can think of the Ones Who Were as symbiotes in this regard. What makes it possible for the Ones Who Were to share knowledge with Shelby is a symbiotic relationship of conceptualization. Your concepts and Shelby's are not the same, but you are aware of the differences. Now, when a human sees a chair, let's say, the human has a concept of that chair's . . . chairness, for lack of a better way of expressing it. Between the time that the chair is seen, perceived as existing, and the time that empirical evidence of its existence is acknowledged by the human's saying 'chair', the concept of the chair must be recognized. Think of it as a process taking place in steps, but taking place with a great deal of speed. The eye *sees* the object. Step one. The message is sent to the brain, the image is translated into a concept. That concept is chair. Step two. Then a message must be sent from the cortex, the center of conceptualization, to the motor system, enabling the brain to give the order for the mouth to say the word 'chair.' Step three. We can break it down further, but it's not necessary. Are you with me so far?"

"Yes, Sean."

"Now, here's where I think the difference comes in. Let's use hellhounds as an example, since you brought it up. Shelby's eye sees the hellhound. The message is sent, the image is conceptualized, now that image is about to be expressed. Only there is a difference between the Shade concept of a hellhound and a human concept of a hellhound,

66

at least in language, if in nothing else. If the Shade concept is given to the motor center to translate, it cannot do so properly, so there must, at that point, occur an *overlapping* of Shade and human concepts. If I can isolate those conceptual differences, if you can put Shelby into a thought-free stasis, I can monitor the conceptual functions of the Ones Who Were and graph them. Once I've accomplished that, I'll be able to program the wave differences into the computer. Having already programmed the computer with Shelby's pre-merged EEG patterns, we'll be able to sort out the various impulses, digitalize them, and assign sound values." He was getting excited. "I can put the different waves up on the screen. There will have to be areas where they intersect, or at least come close. That will give us an audio range from which to work. Then the computer can look for the appropriate sound values to match the wave difference. I could say, for example, the word 'hellhound' to Shelby, then monitor her concept of a hellhound and graph it as a wave. Translate that into acoustical speech with the computer in the same way that an audio signal can be sampled, digitalized, and then duplicated, changed, delayed, whatever. Then you put Shelby into this thoughtless sleep and I run the same experiment with you, graph your concept of a hellhound, and, working from the audio basis we already have from Shelby's concept, seek the right sound values that would match your wave. And we'll have the sound that Shades make when they articulate the concept of a hellhound."

"Do you think it will work?" said Shelby.

"In theory, it should," said McEnroe. "Let's get started."

"But I thought you were tired."

"Fuck that, I'm wide awake. Let's get cracking. We've wasted enough time!"


"Paul, I need to talk to you."

"Sure, Jake, come on in. I was just finishing up here." Paul turned off his desk terminal. "Just trying to get my own files organized. What can I do for you?"

"Have you had a chance to speak to Shelby yet?" said Jake.

"Some," said Paul. "We haven't had time for any in-depth discussions, if that's what you mean. She's been spending almost all her time with McEnroe, working on that language program."

"Well, that's important, but I think something just came up that may take precedence."

"Such as?"

"Rivers and Solaway want to get married," Jake said.

Paul grinned. "That's a problem?"

"It is when they want to have children."

"Oh. I see."

"The Directorate never gave me any guidelines on that one," Jake said. "Ordinarily, it would be out of the question, but this isn't an ordinary situation. It's not as if they're just serving a field hitch on Boomerang, they're probably going to be here for the rest of their lives. I don't know if I have the right to deny them. I have the authority, but I don't know if I have the right."

"And if they're given the right to procreate," said Paul, "then you can't deny it to others, and then we no longer have just a research installation. We've got a colony."

"Precisely."

Paul compressed his lips. "According to ColCom records, Boomerang is not suitable for human colonization."

"Well, we all know what that really means, don't we?" said Jake.

"True, but in the legal sense, it gives you grounds to—"

"I'm not *talking* about the legal sense, Paul. We're here. We're going to *stay* here. I don't think that most of us have really faced that yet. There's been such a relaxed atmosphere around here, only McEnroe and Shelby have been working at a frenzied pitch. He knows nothing but his work and doesn't give a damn for anything else. He could be on an asteroid for all he cares; so long as he's got his work, he's happy. And Shelby's got a vested interest in finding a way to communicate with the Shades. In a sense, they are her people. But the rest of us? Life's been pretty easy for us here. There's a sense of having all the time in the world—you said it yourself when you arrived, the base feels like a resort. But what happens when we get old, Paul? Is ColCom going to take care of us then? They going to bring us all home or what? I don't really know."

Paul nodded. "We *are* a colony, in a sense. The question is, can we allow ourselves to expand? Fannon said a human colony would destroy the Shades."

"It might," said Jake. "He'd know more about them than anyone else except for Nils and, of course, Shelby. That's why I think we've all got to get together and talk about it."

"Don't you think this is something that should be cleared through the Directorate first?" said Paul.

"I think we should know exactly what we're talking about

68

before you and I bring it up before the Directorate," said Jake. "We're not going back anytime soon. I've got to tell these people something before then. We've got to consider all the possibilities. Is this the kind of situation in which we can really consider bringing up children?"

"My immediate reaction would be no," said Paul. "There are still too many variables in our situation. Let's assume that we *are* to remain here for the remainder of our lives. In order for our offspring to have any chance at survival here, we're going to have to make a conscious effort to produce enough of them to make their chances viable. We're going to have to set up programs to take care of and educate them. We're going to have to become even more self-sufficient. We're still very heavily dependent upon ColCom for supplies. It would involve a group effort and a not inconsiderable amount of work. On the other hand, we still have a great deal to learn about this world. And there is the possibility, and it is a very real possibility, that due either to a change in the climate of opinion in ColCom or to something that we learn here if we're successful in setting up communication with the Shades, the project might become declassified. Then we might all be leaving. If it's been established that a human colony here would be destructive to the Shades, as Nils and Fannon seem to believe, then that's a very real consideration."

"We can't threaten the Shades in any way," said Jake.

"Not to play devil's advocate, but we're already a threat," said Paul. "Our presence here has already affected the lives of those Shades in this vicinity, and if we are able to find a way of communicating with them, we'll affect their lives even further. We've got some heavy responsibility here."

Jake sighed. "Tell that to Rivers and Solaway. I don't really want the job."

"There's nothing to prevent their getting married," Paul said. "But I think you're right. This is something that could seriously affect the morale here. Set up a meeting with Shelby, Fannon, Nils, yourself, and me. The Directors obviously haven't thought this whole thing through. We're going to have to do their job for them."

Fannon stirred restlessly in bed. He turned over and saw her watching him. "Shelby?"

"She sleeps," the Great Hunter said.

Fannon turned away in disgust, lying on his side with his back to her. "K'ural," he muttered.

69

The Shade entity made no reply.

He had come to her room several hours earlier. They had talked, she had told him excitedly about the breakthrough they were on the verge of making in reproducing the language of the Shades, and then they had made love.

They made love with less frequency now than they had before. They slept in separate rooms. Fannon did not come to visit her as often as he used to and she never came to visit him. They never spoke about it.

"I just can't get used to her lying there with her eyes open all night," Fannon said, sitll not facing her. "God knows, I've tried, but I can't."

"It is our Way," K'ural said quietly.

"Yes, right, the Great Hunter must watch and protect," said Fannon bitterly. "Who are you protecting her from? Me? You think some hellhound's going to slink through the field, get inside this building and through that door? Do you?"

K'ural did not respond. Instead, the Great Mother entity addressed him. She spoke with Shelby's voice and even though the voice was Shelby's, it sounded different somehow. It was softer than the voice with which K'ural spoke, although it was the same, and it was older, infinitely older, than the voice which Shelby spoke, although it was the same. Unsettlingly the same.

"Why can you not accept what is, Drew?" N'lia said.

"Why can't all of you just leave me alone?" said Fannon.

"Drew—"

"Don't call me that."

He got up out of bed, started to get dressed. As he was putting on his pants, he noticed that Shelby was sitting up in bed and looking at him.

"The One That Is has a memory," said S'eri the Healer. "It is a small memory, but a strong one. It is small because it has been made small, pushed aside. It is a memory of another human for whom the One That Is felt love. This man hurt her. In some ways, this man resembled you, Fannon. It is this memory, and others like it, that turned the One That Is away from others of her kind, made her seek out a life of isolation as the pilot of a ship, made her feel weak and frightened in the presence of other humans like herself. That entity exists no longer. Shelby is the One That Is now. The One That Is can still be hurt. We can make the pain a smaller thing. We can soothe it. We can even make the One That Is forget. But what of *your* pain, Fannon?"

Fannon finished dressing and left without replying.

Paul lay awake in his room. Insomnia had never been a problem with him before, but lately he found it more and more difficult to fall asleep. There was simply too much to think about. He could not turn off the white noise in his brain.

When he had arrived, the foundation of Boomerang Base had appeared strong. Now cracks were forming. They had been forming all along, but it had taken him a while to see them. Fannon was wound up tighter than a drum. McEnroe sought escape from contemplation of his situation in his work. He resented even the slightest interruption, and his surly demeanor was a way of keeping people at bay, just as surely as Fannon preferring to be called by his last name was a subtle distancing defense mechanism. Nils Björnsen dwelt on the problems of others to the exclusion of his own, and he seemed to almost welcome the occasional reception of an empathic projection from a Shade, as if it made it all right for him to settle into his own brand of melancholia. Jake . . .

Jake Thorsen was a slightly different story. Jake was a fatalist who had resigned himself to a desperate retirement until the Boomerang mission came along. The base commander was senior to the others not only in rank, but in age as well. Despite his gray hair and chunky physique, he was fit, but he was unwilling to fully accept the responsibility of his command. In most matters, he deferred to Shelby, using her Touch-acquired knowledge and experience as an excuse. Now, in the matter of Solaway and Rivers, he had come to Paul, as if his status as base psychiatrist automatically qualified him to make such a decision.

And what exactly *was* his status? He had thought originally that he had been sent to make a study of the Shades, to work through Shelby until communication with the natives was established. But he had yet to venture beyond the base perimeter and he had yet to see a Shade. He did not count Shelby and was uncertain if he should. *The men and women on Boomerang are subject to unique pressures.* The words came back to him again and again. Is that why they sent me here? he kept asking himself. To keep these people sane, to keep them functional? Was it to make their isolation sit easier upon the consciences of the Directorate? Or was there some validity to Fannon's suspicion that they wanted something? And if so, what was it? He could not help the feeling that there was something about their situation that he did not know, that possibly none of them knew. He recalled what Jake had said, that none of them had fully realized that they

71

would most likely remain on Boomerang for the remainder of their lives. There was a possibility that the mission would become declassified, even though the Directors had not admitted that possibility. He realized that all the people on Boomerang held on to that hope, just as he did. Boomerang was a beautiful world, but it was not home. To Shelby, perhaps it was, but not to any of the others. For the first time, Paul began to understand what it felt like to be stationed at a hardship post. So many of the SEPAP cases, which he had judged dispassionately, now took on a more intimate degree of significance.

We *are* a colony, he thought. The sooner they accepted that, the better off they would be. A colony whose options were severely limited. He would have to find a way to help them maintain a balance within those limits. Their welfare was his responsibility. But whose was his?

They met immediately after first mess in Jake's room. Shelby had been reluctant to come, since McEnroe was in the process of implementing his new approach to breaking the language. Paul appreciated just how important that was to her. She wanted desperately to be able to communicate with the Shades. For her, nothing else was as important.

"Shelby, I'm very glad you're here," said Paul, who had taken charge of the meeting following a few remarks from Jake. They all knew why they were there. Everyone on the base was aware of the situation. "I think it's going to be very helpful to have a Shade perspective on this situation. I've given it a great deal of thought and I have some ideas on the subject.

"To begin with, I'm not sure that any of us really appreciate the severity of this problem. Susan Rivers did not *have* to come to Jake about this. She and Mose Solaway could have very easily stopped practicing birth control. Both are on medication to control their fertility, as are all the personnel here with the exception of those who have been voluntarily sterilized. That gives us a group of people who are potentially fertile. Susan could have become pregnant without discussing it with anyone except Mose. The periodic medicals would have revealed her pregnancy, but then we would have been faced with the dilemma of whether or not to prevail upon her to abort the fetus. She knew this. I see her coming to Jake not so much as asking permission as it is testing the waters, so to speak. Also, as a method of rebellion."

Fannon frowned. "Rebellion? I don't see that. Rebellion against what? Jake's authority?"

72

"No," said Paul, "rebellion against our situation here. Since I've arrived, I've had a chance to interview all the personnel with the exception of Shelby and Sean McEnroe, who have been cloistered in Heuristics almost constantly. I think that we can divide the personnel into several groups as regards their feelings about being on Boomerang. There is one group of people who have been happy to be here from the beginning. A very small group. There is another group who fall into a sort of fatalistic category. In other words, they had no choice about being sent here, but they accept that as one of the vagaries of a career in ColCom, something that comes with the territory. They would be happier being in a less restrictive situation, but they're not and they've accepted it with a stoic indifference. Not the healthiest attitude. This is a somewhat larger grouping. We have two groups left. Our largest group is composed of people who are not at all happy about being here. They might not have minded a limited hitch on Boomerang, but the very real possibility that they will never leave is something they regard as unacceptable. They see themselves as being stuck here and there's nothing they can do about it. But rather than accept the situation, they avoid confronting it, channeling their energies into other directions and nurturing the hope that something in the situation will change, that the project will eventually become declassified and they will be able to leave. Given the facts of our current situation, this is not likely to happen. It is, of course, a possibility, but odds are against it presently. Failure to realize that poses a danger to mental stability. Then we have our final grouping. This group, also, is very small, but it presents the greatest danger. These are people who actively resent having been sent to Boomerang. They would not be happy here under any circumstances. Right now, there seems to be nothing they can do about it, but they would stop at nothing if they thought there was a chance to leave. These are the individuals who are subject to the greatest degree of stress, and, as such, they pose the greatest threat. Both Susan Rivers and Mose Solaway fall into this latter category, and I think it is significant that they have become pair-bonded."

"Which category do you fit into, Paul?" said Fannon.

"Fair enough," said Paul. "I seem to be in an overlapping situation between the first and third groups, though I'm not the best person to analyze my own motivations. I'm happy to be here, glad for the opportunity, but I would prefer that the mission be declassified for a variety of reasons, among which is the fact that it would present me with more options."

73

"What about the rest of us?" Fannon said.

"Any objections?" said Paul. No one had any. "Very well. Shelby, obviously, fits into the first group. Nils, you're in the second, as is Jake, but to a lesser degree. Fannon . . . you fall into the final category, along with Solaway and Rivers."

"You see me as posing a threat to the stability of Boomerang Base?" said Fannon, honestly surprised.

Paul answered very matter-of-factly. "You asked. Let's just say I see the potential. Right now, though, we're concerned with a more immediate problem. Any action we take regarding Rivers and Solaway must be very carefully considered, as it will affect everyone directly. If we decide that they should be allowed to procreate—and they have made that our decision—we will have established two very important precedents. Both are rebellion-oriented. In the simple act of bringing up the matter, Rivers and Solaway have placed us in an antagonistic position. We lose either way. Whether we decide that they should procreate or not, we are already in the position of the autocratic body, directly exerting a controlling influence on a very intimate aspect of the lives of our personnel. We have already been segregated from them in that regard. If we decide they cannot procreate, there is no way that we can enforce that decision without being dictatorial in the extreme. Our options then would be cut-and-dried. We either enforce the birth-control program as a part of the periodic medicals, thereby taking it out of the hands of our people, or we prevail upon Solaway and Rivers to undergo sterilization, or we prevail upon Rivers to abort the fetus should she decide to become pregnant regardless of what we say."

"No way," said Nils.

"I agree," said Paul. "I'm simply presenting the situation with all its variables. But I should point out that no matter *what* we decide, the very fact of our deciding will have established a precedent of an extreme authority on our part. It's unavoidable. In that respect, their rebellion has been a successful one already."

"You mentioned setting two precedents," said Nils.

"Yes, I did," said Paul. "The second would apply only in the event we decided that they should be allowed to procreate. In so deciding, *we* would then have taken a rebellious action. Boomerang's legal status with ColCom is as not being suitable for colonization. We are not technically a colony. Expanding our population without authority from the Directorate would be an act of mutiny against ColCom and, indirectly, an act of hostility against the Shades, to say nothing

74

of the problems involved with raising children in our present situation."

"Why don't we simply pass the buck?" said Fannon. "Make it the Directorate's decision."

"Unfortunately, that doesn't get us off the hook," said Paul. "It would mean telling Rivers and Solaway that they must postpone any action until Jake and I have a chance to confer with the Directorate. Again, we're in a position of rather extreme authority. Technically, Jake is within his bounds on that account, but the less authoritarian he is, the better for the project. And then, of course, the Directorate would probably refuse, and once again, *we* would be in the position of having to enforce their decision."

"Looks like we're caught between a rock and a hard place," said Jake.

"Can't we simply discuss the whole thing with them, convince them that having children is unwise?" said Nils. "Then it would be *their* decision and not ours."

"Not really," Paul said. "By now the whole base knows that they want to marry and have children. They're waiting to see what we will do. If we discuss the matter with them as you suggest, Nils, and *if* we can talk them into not procreating, it will still be seen as an action taken *by* us."

"So what are we supposed to do?" said Jake. "Not act?"

"No, obviously we can't do that," said Paul. "We've got to accept the fact that *any* action we take is going to damage the social structure of the base in that a large aspect of the communal spirit will be eroded. It will no longer be a case of 'we're all in this together.' The reality of our situation is that we are a paramilitary research installation. Technically. Up till now, the base has been functioning more along the lines of a civilian scientific compound, a semiautonomous democratic enclave. That has made life here a great deal easier. This will be like a rude slap in the face. It will also force many of our personnel to fully confront their situation here, which, as I have already said, many of them have been avoiding."

"Shelby, you haven't said anything," said Jake.

"I'm not sure I have the right to," she said quietly.

"You're affected by this as much as any of us," Fannon said.

"More, in fact," said Jake.

"I understand the problem," Shelby said. "but it's almost impossible for me to be judgmental here. I am potentially fertile. I am also susceptible to the Need. I've only experienced it once before. My Shade aspects understand human sexual-

75

ity, but I'm still capable of going into heat, because of them. I'm not quite certain how I'm going to handle that when it occurs again, as it will before too long. I had hoped to have a means of communicating with the Shades by then, since it is the only time they gather together. I am aware of the fact that expansion of our population would adversely affect the Shades at this point, but I am also aware of the strong procreative instinct of the Shades. I'm torn between the two."

"We can't deny that our presence here hasn't already affected the Shades adversely," Paul said. "They've become even more shy of us, if anything. According to the field-party reports they've drawn back quite a distance from the base. We've taken over a large area of their domain, simply by their withdrawal."

"What would happen if we put it to a democratic vote of the entire base?" said Fannon.

"Can we afford to?" Paul said.

"Why not? If they decided against procreation, they would still be forcing their wishes upon Rivers and Solaway, but in a democracy, a minority is always oppressed by the majority. And we wouldn't be in the position of being made the bad guys. We could hold a meeting, state our case and our reasons against procreation, give them time to think about it, and then vote. And they could also vote on a way to enforce their decision."

"Suppose they voted in favor of procreation?" said Paul.

"What do you think the chances of that are, based on your professional assessment of our personnel?" said Jake.

"I can only guess," said Paul, "and I'd rather not."

"Well, suppose they did vote in favor of another generation," Fannon said. "They won't *all* necessarily immediately start having babies, but even if they do, what of it?"

"What of it?" said Paul. "Well, as I've already pointed out, it would technically constitute mutiny against ColCom and would endanger the project as it would be a potentially—not even that, a *definitely* hostile action against the Shades in that our expansion would continue to displace them from their domains."

"And that would have to be reported to the Directorate," said Fannon. "And what do you think they'd do about it?"

"I'm afraid I see what you may be getting at," said Paul. "You think they might respond by ordering some of us off-planet, those with children."

"And won't that just be a damn shame?" said Fannon.

Shelby gave him a haunted look, but he either didn't see it or ignored it.

"I would suggest that it might not be wise to attempt to second-guess the Directorate," said Paul.

"Well, you would say that, wouldn't you?" said Fannon. "After all, they picked you for this assignment."

"I think that's out of line, Drew," said Nils.

Fannon sighed. "All right. Maybe it is. I'm sorry. But do you see any other way?"

"I'm afraid I don't," admitted Paul.

"Well then, why don't we just let the people decide?" said Fannon. "It does get us off the hook, doesn't it?"

Paul nodded. "Yes, it does." Then, in a voice so soft as to be almost audible, he said something only Jake and Shelby heard, Jake because he was right next to him and Shelby because of her unusually well-developed senses. He said, "You're in the last group, all right."

# CHAPTER EIGHT

The time of Need was also a time of hunting. Shade hunting. The Seedling children had traveled far, to the base of the towering mountains, there to celebrate, there to wait, there to hunt. And there to choose their mates. Mary led the party. She was a tall, wild creature with long brown hair that cascaded down almost to her knees. During forays into the brush, she would tie it back with several strips of dried skin so that it made a thick cord down her back. She was dressed in animal skins, and on her feet were knee-high boots made from the fur and hide of hellhounds. She was human. She looked human. But she thought of herself as a Seedling, a creature sent from the All Father, a being descended from the stars.

They had journeyed together to the base of the mountains, where the age-old trail led up into rock, higher than the clouds, to the canyon of the Spring of Life. There, in the box canyon heated by the bubbling pools, the Shades congregated during the time of Need. None of the Seedling children had ever been to the canyon, but each had memories of the choosing from their parents. Each of them could recall past journeys up into the freezing heights, the hard climb along twisting and treacherous mountain trails to the summit of the lower peaks and across to where the trails joined from the other side. They remembered the fearsome winds that howled in the chasm, threatening to suck them off the ledge that skirted the bottomless gorge. They recalled the awesome bridge of stone and the cavern entrance to the canyon with its sheer walls and volcanic warmth. All this they remembered from the Shades whom their parents had killed and merged with, and when the time of Need came, they longed to go up into the mountains once again, though they had never been before. Still, they did not go. It was not yet time.

Mary knew that the day would come when Seedlings would make that journey. They would go *en masse*, making the dangerous climb that led to the canyon of the Spring of Life. Some of them would die. Those who were strong, those who deserved to survive, would not die. They would make it to the canyon, and there they would fall upon the Shades, turning their Ritual of Choosing and reaffirmation of the Way into a bloody Ritual of Transformation. They would not kill all of them, but they would kill many. They would disrupt the mating cycle of the Shades, making their presence felt in their most sacred place. Ignorant of the will of the All Father, the Shades would fight and flee, but those who would be killed would learn the joy of Transformation, would ascend to a new plane. After that, it would be a time of wild copulation, a time of releasing the pent-up energies that had been partially released by killing, and then they would begin to make their presence felt in the land beyond the mountains, where no Seedling had yet ventured. Mary longed for that day, but she did not know when it would come. Perhaps it would come within a few more years, when there were more of them. Perhaps it would not come within her lifetime as the One That Is. But it would come. When it came, Great Mother Wendy would let all of them know.

For now, they waited. When they felt the time of Need approach, the youngest among them would prepare to make their journey. They would travel to the mountains, where the trails led up to the canyon of the Spring of Life, and they would wait. They would make camp and keep a careful watch as Shades began to travel up into the mountains. They would mate, knowing that soon all of them would merge. And when the Shades came down from the mountains, they would kill them. For all the Seedlings, this would be their first kill and their last. It would mark their passage into adulthood.

Mary was several generations removed from the original Seedlings, descended from Wendy and James. She was an example of the survival of the fittest. James had not survived. He had died the true death, a victim of a hellhound. His son and Wendy's, Drew, had killed his Shade and merged, then married Lani, who had become one of the most skilled hunters of the tribe. When the body of Drew's mother died, Wendy merged with him. Lani also killed her Shade and merged, then merged a second time upon her death, living on as one of the Ones Who Were within the body of her son, Devon. Devon also killed his Shade and was transformed, then fathered a daughter who took on the spirit of her grandfather upon his death. So the line continued.

The experiment was working well, much more successfully than the Directorate could have foreseen. The ability to merge, to give the Touch, was passed on with the joining of a human with the Ones Who Were. From the first time that they killed their Shades and were transformed, the Seedlings had it.

There was a strong imperative to procreate. Each Seedling couple produced as many offspring as was possible. All these children maintained, until the moment of their transformation and passage into adulthood, an esper link with their parents. At the moment of their merging, this link was broken. Each child had to make its own peace with the Ones Who Were. Still, the esper faculty bred true. With succeeding generations, the parental link became stronger until eventually the break between parent and child upon transformation was only a temporary one, overcome by the turmoil of the merging, yet restored when reintegration was complete. By stages and by constant augmentation of added Shade personae, this faculty grew stronger, became more developed. An entirely new race was being born as the genocide of an older one progressed.

The village was much larger now. The Seedlings claimed an ever increasing area as their domain. The Sturmann poles were useless now, the generators powering the field having fallen into disrepair. The buildings used by the original settlers still stood, but they were weathered and crumbling into ruin, many of them damaged by a fierce storm that had hit the village. It was as it should be; the Directorate had intended the Seedlings to go native. The only remnant of the original base that still had any meaning for the Seedlings was the shuttle, the lighter that had brought the first Seedlings down from their doomed ship. It alone was maintained, kept from being overgrown with vines, cleaned inside and out although it would never fly again. It was kept as a shrine, a memorial of how the Seedlings had descended from the stars.

Mary was anxious to get back to the village, not because she was not eager for what lay ahead, but because she knew that when she returned with the other members of the hunting party, they would no longer be treated as children. They would take their place in the community as adults. In one sense, her schooling would be over; in another, it would just begin. She would return transformed, with her own Ones Who Were to tame, with her own mate.

She had chosen Peter. In the Shade mating patterns, the females did the choosing. Among Seedlings, the pattern had been only slightly modified. The females, having the greatest investment in the birth process, sought to mate with the strongest available males, both to ensure a strong and healthy offspring and to protect them during the time of pregnancy when they would be most vulnerable. Among the younger Seedlings, the older and stronger females had first choice. Mary had settled upon Peter, a tall and muscular sixteen-year-old with green eyes and a thick blond mane. Peter was the strongest and most able of all the young males in their party, and with the time of Need at hand, Mary's desire for him was strong. So was Sonja's. As Mary leaned casually against a tree, watching Peter sharpening his spear, Sonja sensed her lust.

Mary felt the empathic projection of someone's aggressive resentment and looked away from Peter to see Sonja staring at her malevolently. Peter was aware of what was going on, but he kept his eyes averted, concentrating on the task at hand. He had no say in the matter. Both Sonja and Mary were very close to him and he would accept whichever way the choosing went, but he had a hope that he kept hidden. He hoped it would be Mary.

"He's mine," said Sonja, advancing. "I have chosen him already. Find yourself another, Mary."

"The choice is mine to make before yours," Mary said lightly.

"I am the oldest," Sonja said. "I am sixteen and you are only fourteen. First choice is mine."

"But I lead the hunt," said Mary.

"Only because you are descended from Great Mother Wendy," Sonja said.

"Because I am the strongest."

"You will have to prove that," Sonja said. "I challenge you."

"I accept your challenge."

"Peter," Sonja said, and for the first time he openly acknowledged his role in the matter, "you decide. How shall we compete?"

A momentary expression of concern flickered across his features. He did not wish to see either of them hurt. And there was still the hunt ahead for them to consider.

"You could throw spears at a target," he suggested.

"The test should be one of strength, not accuracy," Sonja said. "I think we should fight."

The other members of the hunt had gathered all around them, anxious to see the contest, their tempers fired by the Need. They all wanted to pair off as well, but there could be no choosing until Mary and Sonja settled their disagreement. Peter did not want to see them pounding at each other, biting and scratching in the forest clearing. Open wounds, even small cuts, could easily result in infection, and although Healers were able to cure most such, it was not desirable. He thought a moment, then took two of the spare spears that they had brought and knocked the heads off, making light but strong wooden staffs. He handed one to each.

"Very well, then. If you must fight, then fight. Only no blows above the shoulders and no stabbing or poking with the ends. The first to drop her weapon or be unable to continue is the loser."

The conditions agreed upon, Mary and Sonja retired to opposite sides of the clearing and awaited Peter's signal to begin. He merely nodded, standing by with his spear, ready to strike their staffs up in case they should become carried away and forget the rules.

Mary and Sonja advanced slowly, circling each other at a short distance in the center of the circle of onlookers, each keeping just out of the other's reach. Sonja darted in quickly, holding her staff near the end and making a wide sweep at Mary's ankles. Mary stabbed her staff hard into the ground, blocking the sweep, and used it to swing herself up and out at Sonja, kicking her with both feet in the chest. Sonja fell to the ground, but retained her staff. She swung it up to block Mary's sideways blow at her midsection, then lashed out at

81

Mary with her feet, scissoring her just above the ankles and toppling her to the ground. They both regained their footing and started circling once again, breathing hard.

Several times, Sonja would leap in and a quick flurry of strikes and parries would be exchanged, with neither scoring a telling blow. Mary held back, allowing her opponent to come to her, watching and waiting for an opportunity. Sonja soon began to tire. The older girl had expended a great deal more energy during the fight, angered by the fact that her age had not guaranteed her supremacy. She took the fight to Mary and thereby lost it, for the younger girl was stronger, physically smaller, but more muscular and possessed of greater agility. When Mary perceived that her opponent was weakening, she pressed the attack, raining blow after blow upon Sonja's staff, causing the force to be transmitted through the staff to Sonja's hands, not giving her a chance to rest. The fight ended when Sonja, unable to withstand the battering, could no longer hold onto her staff and dropped it to the ground after one of Mary's blows.

It ended there, quickly and without rancor. Sonja was forced to recognize Mary's superior strength, which gave her claim to Peter precedence. As Sonja took time to rest and give consideration to her second choice, Mary and Peter paired off as mates for life. There was no formal ritual. There was no marriage among the Seedlings, nor was there divorce. Simplicity was the key to their existence and the structure of their tribe.

Mary sensed Peter's pleasure and pride in her victory and smiled. She had always liked him. As small children, there had already been a special closeness between them, and she had known somehow, even then, that he would be her mate. Now it had come to pass. They were children no longer. Soon the Shades would begin to come down from the mountains and they would start their hunt. Soon they would become transformed into adults. For now, they still felt the Need within them. Now they could give in to it. Wordlessly, they went to the small shelter Peter had constructed from young saplings, leaving the other members of their party to their own choosing.

In the darkness of the shelter, lit only by the thin shafts of light which broke through the intertwining boughs that made the roof, they shed their skins. Kneeling, they held each other, their fingers touching gently and exploring, their mouths meeting in a long and languid kiss. Mary ran her hands all over Peter's body, feeling the firmness of his muscles, the hardness between his legs. He would make a good father. Together they would produce strong and healthy Seedlings.

The sensations were all new to them, but they knew what to do. Their schooling in the matter had been quite complete. Before leaving for their journey, each of the Seedling children had shared memories of mating with their parents. They had learned, in this manner, not only the mechanics of mating, but the emotions as well. Mary had experienced, through the esper link with her parents, the sensations mating had produced in both her mother and her father, as had Peter. Each knew what it would be like for the other. Their coupling was graceful, slow and natural. They sank down onto the soft bed that Peter had made for them from large leaves and moss. Mary straddled Peter and slowly lowered herself upon him, feeling a momentary resistance and then a brief pain as her hymen broke. For a time, she sat still without moving, simply contracting her vaginal muscles, feeling him inside her. She felt his hands caress the fullness of her hips and then move up to stroke her budding breasts. Slowly, they began to move together, finding their own rhythm, at first looking at each other and smiling at the pleasure they were sharing, then closing their eyes and abandoning themselves to it. They allowed the Need to wash over them completely, and, much later, both wet and still connected, they lay in one another's arms, kissing softly, bestowing lingering caresses on each other and hoping that from the very first, the All Father would bless them with a Seedling of their own.

The hunt was on.

As the Shades came down the mountain trails, they were set upon by the Seedling party. Some were killed immediately, others were pursued as they attempted to escape and were either caught and cut down or fell victim to the traps set by the Seedling children during the time that they had waited for the Shades to begin their descent. The Shades stepped into snares that snapped them up into the air to dangle helplessly upside down until their pursuers came upon them; they were chased into pits that had been covered over and they fell down into them, upon the sharpened stakes. They were felled by spears thrown with unerring accuracy, or they were physically brought down and slaughtered. The Seedling children were careful to kill only as many as they needed, One Shade for each of them. The few that had been trapped by nonlethal snares and were not needed were released, to be harvested another time. They fled into the forest, knowing now that they had yet another natural enemy, one that was much more fearsome than the deadly hellhounds.

The time of Transformation was the most difficult period in the existence of a Seedling child. It was a time of vulnerability. It took some time for them to become reintegrated as adults, with Ones Who Were of their very own. They had to come to terms with the entities that they had taken by force from living Shades. These entities, these Ones Who Were, terrified and confused by what had happened to them, needed time to become accustomed to the beings in whom they were now contained. They had to realize that what had happened to them had been the will of the All Father, that it was yet another test their god had imposed upon them, a test that was a part of the ongoing transformation of their race. Within each Seedling child, a metamorphosis took place.

Mary had looked down at the Shade thrashing in the pit, its every movement sending the sharpened stakes deeper and deeper into its body. The Shade's lips frothed with bloody foam as its head jerked back and forth, mouth opened in a soundless scream. Mary reached out quickly to accept the Touch before the true death claimed the Shade. Sometimes Shades died the true death before they could merge with Seedlings. It was regrettable, but it simply meant that they weren't strong enough, that they were not worthy. This one was strong, thought Mary. This one fought bravely against death. She reached down into the pit to claim her Ones Who Were.

With one last convulsive effort, the Shade clamped its fingers around Mary's wrist, almost pulling her down into the pit. Fire lanced into Mary's arm and raced up through her body, exploding into white heat in her brain. Involuntarily, Mary jerked back from the Touch, but she could not break that death grip. Her eyes rolled up and her last conscious memory as an unmerged Seedling was of those spasming fingers clutching at her. So great was the pain of the burning sensation that she was certain that if she looked down at her arm, it would be crisped beyond recognition. Then she broke free.

The pain was greater than she could ever have imagined. She was beyond screaming. Her overloaded systems sought retreat in shock, but retreat was impossible as every nerve fiber burned with the force of an invasion of a staggering amount of psychic energy. For an incandescent moment, she had the sensation of running panic-stricken through the jungle, then of falling as the ground opened up beneath her. For a minute fraction of a second, she felt the stakes penetrating her flesh and then she was swept away into a maelstrom of images, a whirlpool of genetic memory that churned within her, threatening to rip her loose from the moorings of reality. She lived a thousand thousand lifetimes in a nanosecond, and she could not cope with the massive influx of personae. Somewhere, some part of her that was still the Seedling child Mary sent out a silent call for help, a scream that would never pass her lips.

*"Peter!"*

His reply came back to her with the swiftness of a thought.

*"I hear you, Mary."*

His presence in her mind gave her strength. She stopped feeling afraid, she stopped fighting the pain. Instead, she gave in to the experience, accepted the Transformation, sought to create in herself an area of calm, a space where she could gather her self together. The racing images and memories that hurtled through her seemed to slow, to coalesce. It became so that she could isolate them as fragments of an ever present past.

A mating dance. Many Shades gathered together in one place, high in the mountains at the Spring of Life, which bubbled and lit up the canyon with an eerie glow that flickered. The Giver's Sentinel, the moon of Boomerang, passed over the canyon and the rites began. Many bodies, glistening with sweat, moving in a silent dance of courtship, pairing off and coupling on the canyon floor in a mass orgy of copulation. . . .

A challenge for domain. She faced a Shade who sought to claim her territory. As they came together to do combat, the image seemed to blur and she was fighting Sonja to protect her claim to Peter. . . .

She remembered things that she had never done. She remembered giving birth alone, lying down upon the soft moss in a forest clearing, holding her spear tightly in her hands to protect her offspring if some predator should happen by. She remembered dying, both of violent and of natural causes, passing on to other Shades and merging countless times. She felt the alien entities within her, began to differentiate among them. And they, in turn, experienced her as a being unique to their world. They knew her as a Seedling, a creature descended from the stars, a creation come from the All Father to transform the Shades, to make them undergo a brutal test that would bring them closer to the All Father, closer to godliness. They knew her concept of the Transformation and accepted it. It was God's will. The Seedlings were His instrument.

It was getting dark when Mary once again became aware of her surroundings. The predators of Boomerang were beginning their nightly concert. Mary rose to her feet, alert and strong, revitalized. She looked down into the pit at the body of the Shade whose life entities were now within her. Insects were feasting on the coagulated blood; soon scavengers would strip the flesh from the bones.

"Peter?"

"I'm here." His voice was like a caressing whisper in her mind.

She sensed that he was very near. She turned and saw him where he had been sitting with his back against a tree, keeping watch over her. She could sense that he, too, was merged. They were adults now. They had gained their own Ones Who Were. And they had also gained something else.

They looked at each other with wonder, neither yet realizing the enormity of what had happened to them. Several generations of espers had produced highly sensitive Seedlings, capable of sense impressions and perceptions that were the equal of the faculties possessed by the Shades. Now, they were superior. It had taken the merging process, what the Seedlings called the Transformation, to fully release the capability. Mary and Peter were among the first fully telepathic Seedlings.

She heard the Call as they neared the village. "I'm coming, grandmother," Mary sent, not knowing if she would be heard. She and Peter left the others and hurried on ahead.

In the village, an old Seedling woman was dying. She had sent out the Call, knowing intuitively that her granddaughter was nearby, but she had been shocked when a reply came, a reply in the form of an articulated thought.

"I'm coming, grandmother."

The Ones Who Were within her felt pleased. Mary had proved worthy. She had received yet another blessing from the All Father. Soon the newly merged adults arrived, and Mary entered her grandmother's cabin while Peter waited outside respectfully. The old woman spent some time in silence with her daughter and her now adult granddaughter. After a time, she looked at Mary's mother, smiled, and said, "I'm ready."

Mary leaned forward and kissed her grandmother, then the

86

old woman reached out a gnarled hand and touched Mary on the breast. Once again, Mary felt the burning pain of the Touch as the entities within her grandmother and the spirit of the old woman herself passed on to her. She received the human Ones Who Were, Great Mother Wendy and Great Father Drew. Great Hunter Lani became hers, as well. She also received the Shade entities who had retained their dominance since the time of the first merging of Seedling and Shade, S'utar the Healer and D'ali, Father Who Walked in Shadow. Her biological mother held her tightly as Mary writhed from the pain of merging. A moment later, the contact was broken and the merging was complete.

So the line continued.

# CHAPTER NINE

Paul looked at the woman seated before him and felt a strong empathy with Fannon. She was, in the most literal sense, a creature of unearthly beauty. There was no one like her anywhere in the universe. Even though he had grown accustomed to her physical appearance, it was hard not to stare. The silvery-blue skin made a stark contrast with the snow-white hair that framed her face, and the opalescent gaze of her violet eyes seemed to go right through him.

"I've been putting you off, Paul," she said. "I'm sorry."

He shrugged. "Well, that's understandable. Your work with Sean—"

"That's only part of the reason," she said.

"Oh?"

"I know that you've been anxious to start your sessions with me. The thing is, I represent an 'opportunity' for you. I can't blame you, but I was poked and prodded enough to last me a lifetime when I was back at Gamma. You must know that I spent most of my young life in institutions."

Paul nodded. "That's Shelby talking, though. What about the Ones Who Were?"

"We have concerns of our own," she said. Paul did not fail to note the significance of her use of the plural, something she did not do ordinarily. "The merging is both a blessing and a curse. In one sense, it saved our lives. In another, it complicated them almost beyond endurance. The Shades can no longer continue to exist in the same way that they have for ages. They've been discovered by the humans. That changes everything. There must be contact between Shades and humans. The Ones Who Were see it as the will of the All Father. Our human aspect sees it as a simple inevitability.

"The speech analysis program is almost complete. We should be ready to try talking to the Shades within a day or two. They may not want to listen, but at least we know that they'll be able to understand us. What happens then remains to be seen. Sean is working on a device that should enable them to communicate with us, that is, if we can work it out and if the Shades *want* to communicate with us. It would require their cooperation in being hooked up to a sensing unit containing a transducer that would scan their brain waves and translate them into acoustical speech via the analyzing program and the synthesizer. Still, there's no guarantee that it will work. The model was constructed based on the structure of my human brain. We'll have to find a Shade willing to be a laboratory guinea pig. I've been that route myself, and I can't say that a Shade would find the experience any more palatable. Still, at least we'll be able to talk to them. If they'll respond, perhaps it won't be necessary to 'wire them for sound,' as Sean puts it. We might be able to establish a form of sign-language communication, similar to what's been done with Terran primates."

"But?" said Paul.

"But even if we do succeed in establishing communication, we would face still another obstacle and an even greater responsibility," she said. "The Shades have no tribal structure, beyond the self-contained one between the One That Is and the Ones Who Were. It's inevitable that our interaction with them would change that, and who can predict what effect that would have on them as a species? The Ones Who Were see this as an inevitable development intended to occur by the All Father. The One That Is questions whether or not humans have the right to interfere with an already extant culture. It's hard to reconcile those contradictions within my self."

"Maybe I can help," said Paul. "That's what I'm here for."

"With all due respect, Paul, I don't think you're qualified," she said. "If I were human, you would be working with me as though I possessed discrete personalities. But I'm not human and I'm not a case of split personality. I am an *integrated being*. You can't treat the Ones Who Were as a neurosis."

"I had no intention of even making the attempt," said Paul. "I'd be a liar if I didn't admit to an overwhelming scientific curiosity concerning the phenomenon of your merging, but frankly, your own concern is a large part of why I've had my own inhibitions in the matter. My primary role here is concerned with the welfare of the base personnel. I perceive that you have your own internal conflicts, but I believe that you're in a much better position to resolve yours than the rest of the personnel are to resolve theirs, and we *do* have problems."

"I was aware of that," she said, "but I've been so involved in my own work that I'm afraid I've grossly underestimated them."

"Fannon's, too?"

She was silent for a moment. When she spoke, it was very softly. "No. Not Fannon's."

"I'm going to need help, Shelby. I can't handle this alone, and I'm hoping that possibly the Ones Who Were can help me, too. I don't know exactly how, but I've been giving it some thought." He sighed and rubbed the bridge of his nose. "Morale is, to put it bluntly, disastrously low."

"Is it as bad as all that?"

"I'm afraid it is. Things are beginning to fall apart. I've had ample opportunity to observe everyone here, with the exception of yourself and Sean, who's been pretty uncooperative, but leave that for now."

Paul stood and began to pace. He felt a need for movement, as though even the small amount of energy expended in walking back and forth would help to dispel the mounting tension within him.

"You know, sometimes when I'm by myself in this room," he said, "I almost forget where I am. That is, it feels somehow as though I'm not on Boomerang, but back in some office cubicle on an orbital station or in the bowels of ColCom HQ."

He gestured expansively at the walls.

"No windows," he said. "There's a sense of isolation here. And that is precisely the problem, in its most essential form. Isolation. We're not only isolated from human civilization here, we're isolated from our own environment. None of those here have really confronted their situation. They've all built up avoidance mechanisms. McEnroe—and, to an extent, you, too—buries himself in his work to the exclusion of almost all other activity. There's a lot of that going on. When I first arrived, Fannon joked about starting a softball team, but the fact is that no one is recreating. The people here have carved what could amount to a country club out of the wilderness, but no one is using the golf course, to follow the analogy. To a large degree, Boomerang Base is like a minimum-security prison. There are no guards, everyone has all the comforts of home, but it *isn't* home. And we are just as effectively imprisoned here as if there were armed guards all around us. A sense of ennui pervades this place."

He stopped and leaned against a wall, staring at Shelby.

"We're in a Twilight Zone of our own here," he said. "We are supposedly a research installation, and it's true that we are that, but it is equally true that the work is falling off. Some people do nothing but work, and a growing number of others do nothing period. They do nothing because they realize that we are also a prison in a very real sense. Jake and I are the wardens. We're allowed to leave for periods of time while everyone else is doomed to stay here unless something happens to declassify the mission. The people who are working hard are doing so because it helps them not to think about their situation and because they nurture precisely that hope, that we will all be going back someday. Who knows, perhaps that's true. But it's dangerous for them to pin all their hopes on that. Hope, contrary to the bromide, does not spring eternal. Eventually, it dies, and when it does, those who have built everything upon it go all to pieces. There are already signs of stagnation, and there are also signs of rebellion, in Fannon, in Solaway and Rivers, and in others. A rebellious state is the healthier of the two, but that isn't saying much considering our circumstances."

He went back to his desk and sat down heavily.

"Now we are to have this vote on whether or not we should allow ourselves to procreate. I'm afraid I know how that vote will turn out. Yet that's only the first step. Jake is due to make one of his trips back to Gamma 127 before too long. I'll be going with him. That, in itself, separates us from everybody else. There is already some resentment, from Fannon in particular. We're already in a situation where a group of us is seen as an inner circle. I've been here almost a full year and I have yet to see a Shade. I understand that the number of field trips has been cut down, that the extent to which they travel away from the base has been reduced for fear of displacing any more Shades, but at the same time that action has further isolated us from our own mission, from the environment. We've turned into a group of shut-ins."

"The field trips will be resumed, increased in fact, now that we're ready to attempt communication with the Shades," said Shelby. "At least now we can try to explain ourselves to them."

"Yes," said Paul, "it's absolutely vital that we engender a new enthusiasm for the mission among our personnel. But that will solve only part of the problem."

"What do you suggest?"

"I'm afraid that I have no answers," said Paul. "Less than one year since I arrived, and already so much deterioration. We've got to stop it somehow, but ColCom has placed us in an impossible situation. I'll have to take that up with them. I've persuaded Jake to move up our departure date, but that still won't take care of the problem with Rivers and Solaway."

"You think the vote will go in favor of their having children."

"I'm almost certain of it. No one wants to be placed in a position of having to tell someone that they can't have a child."

"Is it really so serious a problem?" Shelby said. "I don't see what harm a few children could do."

"No immediate harm," said Paul, "unless the Directorate categorically forbids it. Then we'll have a real problem on our hands."

"What would happen if you simply didn't tell them about it?" Shelby said.

"They'd have to know eventually," said Paul. "Still, consider the implications. We have a number of potentially fertile people. Even if all of them started procreating right now, it would pose no immediate threat to the Shades. But consider what would happen over a period of time. Our population would continue to expand. We'd become a thriving colony, precisely the thing you and the other members of the original survey team determined would eventually destroy the Shades."

"You're talking about something that would happen quite a few years down the line," said Shelby. "You're making the assumption that our situation here won't change."

"You have reason to believe it will?"

"I think it's bound to. Once we've established communication with the Shades, ColCom would want increased contact between Shades and humans. If strict parameters for that contact could be observed, the Shades should be affected only minimally."

"Perhaps," said Paul. "We've already hurt them by discovering them. But you're forgetting something. There is still the aftermath of the plague drug to contend with."

"Time heals wounds," said Shelby.

"You've never seen a plague child. They won't forget about it quite so soon." Paul sighed. "The preachers have a lot of power now," he said bitterly.

"Fannon had an idea about that," Shelby said.

"He did?"

"You mean he's never mentioned it to you?"

"No, he hasn't."

Shelby licked her lips. "It's one hell of an idea," she said. "He's even discussed it with Jake. He thinks it might be possible for us to go back to Earth's future."

*"What?"*

"Knowing how news of the Shades would be accepted on Earth so soon after the plague drug, Fannon came up with the idea of returning through the Zone to a future time, when the memory would not be so fresh and painful and people might be more receptive to news of a race that lives forever. He feels that they would then be ready to accept the Shades as equals and the people here would be free to decide the course of their own lives."

"That idea's absurd," said Paul. "Fannon's a sleeper. He's not thoroughly familiar with the technology of ghosting."

"Yes, but Jake is."

"Are you telling me that they're *serious* about this?" Paul said incredulously.

Shelby was a little slow in answering. "Drew wants to leave here at all costs," she said. "Jake sees the idea as a theoretical possibility, something that's interesting to think about, a possible last resort."

"Last resort?"

"If we've done everything we can here and they still won't let them return, if the situation here becomes intolerable for them."

"You say 'for them.' What about yourself?"

"Boomerang is home for all but the human aspect of me," she said.

"I see." He took a deep breath. "Has Fannon discussed this with anybody else?"

"Not to my knowledge."

"I'm going to have to have a talk with him. And Jake, too. Jake should know better than to encourage him in something like this. As if we didn't have enough problems. How the hell does he expect to ghost to the future? No one's ever been there before! How can you lock into a mindset of a future time?"

"Jake says that there is no such thing as a future time, that there is only an infinite number of potential futures. It's true that no one's ever attempted anything like that before, at least not so far as anybody knows, but—"

"But Jake is just the one to try it," Paul said. "God, no wonder they get along so well. The two of them were meant for each other. Two risk-taking personalities, strongly aggressive, impulsive . . ." Paul shook his head. "And I'm supposed to hold all this together."

"Is that what you're supposed to do?" said Shelby gently.

"Looks as if it's turning out that way," said Paul. "Maybe that's what the Directors intended all along when they sent me here. Fannon's personality is more volatile than anyone else's, and Jake is encouraging him."

"You don't have to tell me about Drew's personality," she said.

"No, I suppose I don't. But if they were to attempt this mad scheme, where would that leave you?"

"I don't know," she said. "The problem hasn't come up yet, has it? We still have to establish communication with the Shades."

"And you haven't thought beyond that?"

"To be honest, I haven't wanted to."

"You're afraid of losing him, aren't you?" Paul said.

"A part of me is," she said. "Then again, I'm not sure I 'have' him. My human aspect loves him. My Shade aspects empathize with that and understand the human need for it, only Drew is becoming increasingly resentful of the Ones Who Were."

"It's interesting that you keep referring to 'your human aspect' when I hear you denying your humanity," said Paul. "Are you or aren't you?"

"A part of me is," she said. "A greater part of me is not."

"I see. With whom do you feel a greater degree of identification? With Shades? Or with humans?"

She swallowed nervously. "We are both Shade and human, yet we are neither."

"You are also avoiding the question," Paul said. "You suggested earlier that as a psychiatrist my reactions toward you would be as though you possessed a split personality, yet I am more than a psychiatrist. I was also a SEPAP official and, as such, I frequently had to make assessments of human interaction with alien life forms. It might be easier for most of the people here to deal with the phenomenon of what you have become by considering you as being a case of multiple personalities, all of which are in constant interaction. However, as both a psychiatrist and a SEPAP official, I am considerably more flexible. Many of them have had contact with alien life forms, but I've routinely had to analyze far more such contacts then any of them have experienced. I understand that you are unique, a case of gestalt personality, rather than split personality. I know that I can speak directly with any 'one' of you and/or to all of you at once. You said that you don't believe I'm qualified to help you with the contradictions inherent in your existence. I submit to you that I'm the *only* one qualified to do just that. However it is you see yourself, you are the single most important person on this mission, and this mission is in trouble. I just want to make certain I know where your priorities lie."

"You're not being very fair," she said.

"No, I'm not. I am not in the least concerned with being fair or with handling your sensibilities with kid gloves. I suggest to you that you have your own motivations above and beyond this mission and that for that reason, it is important to you to continue reinforcing your concept of yourself as not being human. You've even got the people closest to you believing that. That makes it convenient for you, doesn't it? They're all so careful to avoid offending the Ones Who Were. Ironic that the only one who doesn't completely buy that is Fannon. And you're already making rationalizations to enable you to handle that, to excuse it. Only your 'human aspect' is in love with Fannon. A greater part of you is not, but that greater part 'has empathy.' How nice of them."

"I don't think I care to pursue this discussion any further," she said, getting to her feet.

"I'm afraid you'll have to."

She went to the door. "Open it," she said.

Paul remained at his desk. "I'll open the door when I'm ready."

She walked purposefully over to the desk and reached

across it, her hand moving toward the console that would unlock the door and open it. Paul snatched at her hand, grasping her wrist and preventing her from reaching the console. He held her tightly.

"I said I'll open it when I'm ready."

He looked up into a cold, feral gaze that seemed to burn through him. He felt butterflies forming in his stomach. Björnsen's words came back to him. *The Shadow is strongest at moments of psychic distress.*

"Sit down, T'lan," he said evenly. "You can't stare me down. I'm not a hellhound."

T'lan tore Shelby's wrist from his grasp. Shelby remained standing. Paul realized that it was a dangerous moment. He had to handle it very carefully. Shelby had retreated behind her Shadow aspect, but she had not fled. She was still there.

"I see that I'm perceived as being a threat," said Paul in a steady, forced offhand tone. "Shelby retreats and the compensatory entity comes forth into dominance. The question is, whom am I threatening? The Ones Who Were or Shelby's 'human aspect'? You're not going to attack me, are you, T'lan?"

"The One That Is wishes to leave," T'lan said. "You are preventing it."

"That's quite true," said Paul.

"Why?"

"Because I see it as my duty," said Paul. "Problems are rarely solved by running away and refusing to face them. When you were a One That Is, T'lan, did you run away from threatening situations?"

"No. I felt no fear."

"Which is why you are what you are," said Paul. "Fear can rule a personality if it is not faced."

"You feel fear now," said T'lan. It was Shelby's voice, but it had a chilling quality to it.

"Yes, I do," said Paul. "I haven't met you before, not directly. I find you frankly frightening. But if I opened that door right now, then I would be allowing my fear to rule me, and I'm not going to do that."

"The Ones Who Were will not be ruled by fear," T'lan said.

"I'm relieved to hear that. It isn't my intention to threaten you. All I ask is that you stay and work this out with me. It doesn't matter in the least to me which persona you choose to present. You're still you. I'm only here to help."

Shelby sat down. "The Healer will address the human Healer," S'eri said.

"Whatever makes you feel most comfortable," said Paul, relaxing. He understood what Jake had meant now when he described the encounter with the hellhound. T'lan dominant in Shelby had scared him.

"You think we don't care about the humans?" S'eri said. Her voice was soft now, soothing.

"I didn't say that," Paul said, "nor do I think it."

"What then?"

"You said it yourself," he said, recalling Shelby's words. "You have other concerns. Concerns of a more immediate nature. You want to establish contact with the Shades. The people, as you say. They *are* your people. But we're your people, too. You seem to want to deny that. I don't think it's healthy. The One That Is *is* human. In spite of what you say, in spite of what you have convinced the others to believe. Shelby took on the Ones Who Were in the merging, but that didn't change what Shelby was. It *added* to it. Fannon thinks Shelby is outnumbered. I think he's right."

"You think we are harming the One That Is?" said S'eri. "We would never do that. We are one. We would not harm ourselves."

"And yet you *are* harming the One That Is, in a way," said Paul. "You recall our first conversation, when I addressed K'itar and we spoke about the All Father and doubt?"

"Yes."

"At the time, I wondered what it must be like for you as a gestalt personality to accept something as an irrevocable truth and still doubt it at the same time. I thought it might set up an irreconcilable conflict. But you've handled that already, haven't you? You've prevailed upon the One That Is to go along with what you see as your holy task or whatever to bring Shades and humans together. Well, that's our goal, too, but you've excluded all other considerations."

"It is the will of the All Father—" began S'eri, but Paul interrupted impatiently.

"I don't give a damn about the will of the All Father."

"Blasphemy!"

"Not to me, it isn't. I don't share your faith. I don't believe in the existence of a supreme being. I believe in men, not gods."

As he spoke, he became aware of a growing sense of sadness welling up within him, and it was a moment before he realized that the reaction wasn't his.

96

"Stop it. I don't want or need your pity." Then he realized what had just happened fully. "Well, that's a revelation in itself," he said. "I didn't know that you could do that."

"We did not realize we were projecting," S'eri said. "We apologize. We will attempt to refrain from disturbing you."

"I see I've offended you. Well, you can take it that your single-mindedness of purpose offends me. I begin to wonder just how much you are capable of projecting and to what degree you control it."

S'eri said nothing.

Paul took a deep breath and let it out slowly. "I'll be damned. It was you all along, wasn't it? *You* were doing it!"

It was one of those moments of insight where he was absolutely sure he had it right. And it clicked. The original survey team, according to the mission records, had reported a falling-off in productivity, a gradual dissociation, a feeling of melancholia and detachment that they later learned was due to the psychic projections of the Shades. Supposedly, they weren't aware that they were doing it, it was an unconscious projection, a latent ability they were not in control of, but Shelby's Ones Who Were knew, from their merging with a human and from their experience of others, what effect this unconscious projection of theirs had. And knowing that they did it, they had learned how to exploit it.

"Our presence here was displacing Shades," said Paul. "The more active we were, the farther our field parties went, the more we drove away the Shades."

"They avoid humans only because they do not understand," S'eri said.

"And until we were in a position to attempt to explain things to them, to bring them the truth as you perceive it, the will of the All damnable Father, you did everything you could to slow things down," said Paul. "Shelby worked like crazy on the program while you projected, amplifying everyone's sense of isolation, creating a condition of ennui, protecting the poor ignorant 'people' from the truth until you were ready to give it to them, is that it? Of course. You said it all. 'They've been discovered by the humans. That changes everything.' And Shelby's human aspect went along with it because Shelby doesn't see herself as being human. That *would* make it much more convenient."

"I haven't done anything wrong!" said Shelby. "I haven't changed the way they felt!"

"No, of course you haven't. You couldn't. But you played

97

upon those feelings because it served your purpose. And thanks to you, the Shades have not been interfered with to the same extent they were when I first arrived. Only *we've* been interfered with. No one even suspected you might have had an effect on the morale because no one suspected that you could project."

"I did what I thought I had to do," she said.

"You mean what the 'greater part' of you thought you had to do. You're wrong, Shelby. You're not an integrated being. Your humanity has not been integrated into what you've become. It's been sublimated."

"Don't you see that it doesn't matter?" she said. "We're ready to communicate with them now! They'll be able to see what we are, that we're not a threat. They'll be able to *understand*."

"It doesn't matter?" said Paul. "Tell that to Fannon. Tell it to Nils. Tell it to Jake, who sees himself as having lost control and who's lost his ability to assert himself so that he has to come to others for advice on command decisions. And he comes to you, of course, as well as to me. That makes it convenient, too."

"I had to protect the people, Paul," she said. "I *had* to. Do you think it's fair that we've simply moved in on them, driving them out of their domains, confronting them with a type of creature that they don't understand?"

"No, I don't think it's fair, any more than I think it was fair of you to interfere with the base personnel," said Paul, "but then I told you that I'm not concerned with fairness. If it comes to a choice between protecting our people and protecting the Shades, the Shades are going to lose out. And that's something you're simply going to have to face."

"Are you asking me to choose sides, Paul?"

"I thought you had already made that choice," he said.

"No," she said softly. "All I wanted to do was prevent unnecessary contact. At least until the language program was completed."

"Well, what's done is done," Paul said. "The question is, where do we go from here?"

"Are you going to tell them what I've done?"

Paul snorted. "I don't dare. Right now all I'm concerned with is restoring some sense of *esprit de corps* around here, that and figuring out what to do about the Solaway-and-Rivers vote. And I'm also concerned about you, and I mean all of you, as a gestalt personality, not just your human aspect. Yes, I want you to choose sides, for your own good as well as for everyone else's. And now that I know you're capable of projecting, I have an idea how you can make amends."

# CHAPTER TEN

A new star had appeared in the night sky over Boomerang. Great Mother Wendy told the Seedlings that it was a sign. Soon, very soon, they would gather the largest hunting party ever and attack the Spring of Life. Then they would cross the mountains, to begin spreading throughout the land upon the other side.

The new star was a ship, a sublight survey ship that had brought the original team to Boomerang. There were now two Wendys on the planet. Great Mother Wendy had waited for this event for a thousand years. Beyond the mountains, Nils Björnsen, Drew Fannon, and Wendy Chan were discovering the Shades.

It felt strange to know that she was in two places at the same time. When she first saw the ship in orbit around Boomerang, she remembered all over again what her first trip to Boomerang had been like. The memory was startlingly fresh. As the senior Elder in the Tribal Council of the Seedlings, she had explained many times in the past why they could not cross the mountains until after they had seen the sign. The paradox had to be avoided. Lieutenant Win T'ao Chan could not meet Great Mother Wendy and the Shades who lived beyond the mountains could not know about the Seedlings, for if they knew, then their reactions to the human survey team would not be the same reaction of indifference that the team had reported. Shades who knew the Seedlings knew them as enemies. Seedlings were human. It was essential that history remain unchanged, and the history in question was Wendy's own.

As time went on and the Seedlings watched the new star in

the sky, the events that would lead to their being sent to Boomerang a thousand years ago were taking place. Lieutenant Win T'ao Chan was experiencing for the first time the empathic projections of a Shade and withdrawing into catatonia. Shelby Michaels was being revived from coldsleep to take her place, finding a wounded Shade, a Shade who did not know humans as enemies and so merged with one. Then, one night, the star was no longer making its rapid journey across the heavens and Wendy knew the ship had left. The survey ship which had originally brought her to Boomerang had departed and she was aboard, enshrouded in the sapphire mist of a preserving cryogen. There was no danger now. Nothing they could do would affect their own history. Now they could cross the mountains. Now they could attack the Spring of Life.

"I don't understand," said Fannon. "You're telling me you've changed your minds, just like that? I thought this was so important to you two."

"It was," said Susan Rivers, a slim attractive blonde who worked in the chemistry lab. Sitting next to her, holding her hand, was Mose Solaway, a heavyset xenobiologist who was several years her junior.

They had joined Fannon at his table, asking to speak to him and Jake. It was morning and they had lingered over first mess while most of the other personnel had left to pursue their varied duties.

During the midpoint of the meal, Jake had stood and rapped on the table several times, waiting until everyone settled into silence. He then turned the floor over to Shelby, who announced that they would be resuming their field trips into the bush. The first one, she had said, would be made the next day in order to make the first field test of the speech analyzer program. The field party would consist of herself, Jake Thorsen, Drew Fannon, Nils Björnsen, Mose Solaway, and Paul Tabarde. Sean McEnroe would remain at Boomerang Base with a small support unit to act as communications link with the base and to supervise the computer tie-in. The news had been greeted with enthusiasm, and a feeling of anticipation and excitement swept through the mess hall.

After Shelby made the announcement, she sat down and Jake took the floor again.

"We have another item on our agenda today," he said, "one that's of vital interest to everyone. You're all aware of the controversial proposal made by Susan Rivers and Mose Solaway."

He had paused significantly, and the enthusiasm in the room waned noticeably.

"I'd like to call a meeting of all base personnel here tonight at twenty-one hundred hours in order to discuss it. That's all, people, thank you."

As the meal ended and people began to drift off, Susan Rivers and Mose Solaway had come over to Fannon and Jake, at the table they shared with Paul Tabarde, Nils Björnsen, and Shelby. And now, as they were having coffee, Susan Rivers was expressing doubts as Mose sat by quietly, keeping in the background as usual and allowing her to do most of the talking.

"It was very important to us and it still is," Susan was saying. "We do want to get married and we'd like to have children, but I simply have the feeling that we may be rushing it."

Fannon frowned. "You were so insistent before—what happened?"

She sighed. "I don't know. The decision to call a vote on it—"

"The meeting tonight is simply to discuss it," Fannon said. "I think it's an important step for the base, and all of us should have a chance to talk it over."

"But you *were* going to put it to a vote, weren't you?" she said. "Frankly, I'm not sure how I feel about that. I do know that I suddenly feel pressured."

"Pressured," Fannon repeated. "It wasn't putting pressure on us when you decided that you and Mose wanted to have kids? You were sure then. I still don't know what's made you change your mind."

"Lighten up, Fannon," Jake said. "It's an unusual situation. I think her reaction is understandable in light of the circumstances."

"What about you, Mose?" Fannon said. "How do you feel about it?"

Mose shrugged awkwardly. "I just want what's best for Susan," he said. "And for all of us."

"I see," said Fannon. "So what do you want us to do?"

"I think we should still have the meeting tonight," said Susan. "You know, to talk about it. But I don't want anybody putting it to a vote. I don't think anyone has the right to vote on what I should or shouldn't do with my body."

"Okay, Susan," Jake said. "We'll discuss it, but that's all.

101

No one is going to make any decisions for you. Fair enough?"

She nodded. "Thanks, Jake."

After they had gone, Fannon lit up a cigarette and stared into his coffee for a moment.

"Someone's trying to talk them out of it," he said.

"You sound disappointed," said Paul.

"What's that supposed to mean?"

"Look, let's not get into an argument about this," Jake said. "Personally, I'm relieved that they're having second thoughts. It's a highly volatile situation and I think we should all just take it easy. There are no simple answers."

"I have a feeling you had something to do with this," said Fannon, looking at Paul. "What did you say to them?"

"We haven't even talked about it," Paul said.

"Let's just drop it for now, okay?" said Nils. "The meeting is set for tonight, and everyone can air their views then. Jake's right. There are no simple answers. Let's just concentrate upon one thing at a time. We have the speech analyzer program to put to the test today, so let's just worry about that first, all right?"

"I think that's a good idea," said Jake, getting up. "Fannon, what do you say? You want to help me draw equipment for the trip?"

Fannon nodded, but said nothing. He got up. "Coming, Nils?"

"I think I'll finish my coffee. I'll be along in a moment."

He waited until after Jake and Fannon had gone.

"I'm worried about this meeting tonight," he said.

"So am I," said Paul.

"You know," said Nils, "I had a strange thought before, when you were making the announcement to the personnel, Shelby. A lot of them didn't know that we were ready to test the program today, so they were understandably excited. I knew, though, and the announcement should have been somewhat anticlimactic for me, only it wasn't."

"Enthusiasm is contagious," Paul said.

"Mmmm. Interesting that you should put it that way," said Nils, without taking his eyes off Shelby. "I don't suppose you discussed anything with Susan Rivers and Mose Solaway recently?"

"We talked about the possibility of raising children here," said Shelby.

"I thought as much," said Nils. "You know what it is I'm not saying, don't you? Paul?"

"I'm not sure I follow you," Paul said.

"I'm sure you do," said Nils. "I think what you're doing is very dangerous. I don't think anyone else has guessed that Shelby is capable of projecting just like a Shade. Not yet. It's a very subtle feeling. It's a fascinating development. One that certainly merits further study, don't you think?"

Paul and Shelby were both silent.

"I've suspected it for quite some time now," Nils said, "but I wasn't sure." He pursed his lips thoughtfully and drummed his fingers on the table. "Be careful. If you think we've got problems now, think about what might happen if they realize that they've been manipulated. I'd be especially careful around Drew. He's under a great deal of stress." He took a deep breath and let it out slowly, then rose to his feet. "I think I've made my point."

It was silent in the canyon. Sheltered from the fierce mountain winds, the canyon was a place of warmth, of security. It was a sacred place. The Shades congregated here only during the time of Need, when their normally solitary existence became, for a short while, transformed into a communal ritual of mating. Now it was over. Strange light flickered on the walls. The silence was broken only by the bubbling and hissing of the volcanic pools that gave the Spring of Life its name. Bodies were scattered everywhere.

T'mal was shivering, even though the bubbling pools gave the canyon warmth. He stood not too far from the hissing pool and he could feel the intense heat coming from it, but still he shivered. Within him was a turmoil of fear and confusion as his Ones Who Were attempted to deal with the dreadful reality of what lay before them. T'mal walked slowly, numbly, picking his way among the bodies, stepping over and around torn and bloody corpses. Here one male was sprawled upon the canyon floor, thick white mane matted with blood, entrails spilling out from a wide gash in the stomach. There, lying upon a rock outcropping as if flung there and discarded, a female lolled grotesquely with a spear protruding from her chest. It was a scene of unspeakable carnage, and there was nothing in T'mal's experience to even remotely prepare him to deal with such a sight. Bodies, bodies everywhere and the smell of death. But it was not the true death, and that made it even worse.

The attack had come during the Ritual of Choice. While the people danced, celebrating the way of life, reaffirming their existence and taking joy in the All Father's blessings, the creatures had descended upon them, striking with a force and savagery unlike anything T'mal had ever seen. They were even worse than hellhounds. And hellhounds did not attack in packs. They came down the mountain trails, pouring into the canyon like a swarm of insects, so many of them, more than he could count, all howling like beasts driven mad from hunger. T'mal had never seen such creatures before. Their flesh was different from that of the people, pale like the inside of a river fish. They dressed in skins of beasts and their manes were all different colors. Some had manes upon their faces. Their eyes were dead eyes, no glow of life came from them. Even as they came, the people were all struck with their fury. The Ones Who Were within T'mal had cried out in pain from their onslaught. T'mal had not understood how it was possible for them to cause pain from a distance, and he fled from them, running as fast as he was able up the mountain trail opposite from where they came. He climbed very high above the canyon and hid there behind the rocks, watching with horror as the strange creatures slaughtered all the people. And he had seen a fearsome thing, even more horrible than the slaughter itself. There were many of the creatures, very many. As they attacked, they did so in groups, isolating people from each other, herding them, keeping them apart. Then and only then they killed, forcing the people to choose between true death and a fate as horrible, merging with their killers. T'mal had seen that some of the people had chosen the true death, but many did not, could not. To die, forever, without merging, to condemn generations to eternal nothingness, was so frightening a thought that even merging with a beast seemed preferable, and surely these were beasts of the most savage sort. He thought of the torment of all the Ones Who Were within those beasts, those Ones Who Were Not, and he was filled with pain and fury. How could the All Father have caused such a beast to be? Where had they come from? *Why* had they come?

T'mal stood alone upon the canyon floor, amid all the gory horror, stood shivering with fear and fury, and something cold began to grow within him. T'kar, his Father Who Walked in Shadow, became strong within him, overpowering M'tar, the Great Father, becoming stronger than Great Mother N'tari, who had no soothing maternal advice to give, more dominant than L'sar, the Healer, who could not heal such a frightful wound. Only K'dan, the Great Hunter, did not recoil as did all the others. At that moment, the Shadow and the Hunter welled up within him, fed his fury, grew stronger from his pain. T'mal would have to meet this threat. T'mal had to survive. There was a movement to T'mal's left, and moving with the quickness of a hellhound, T'mal bent down and picked up a spear, turning to meet the threat.

It was not a beast, One Who Was Not. It was one of the people.

It was another young male, like himself. It was probably his first time of Need. For T'mal, it had been only his second mating season. The other young male looked frightened and confused. There was blood on him. He had been wounded, but he had escaped the slaughter. T'mal lowered his spear. He beckoned the young male forward.

They could not speak. Shades were strongly territorial, and except for the time of Need, whenever one trespassed upon the domain of another, they fought to establish dominance. However, what had happened was more than enough to overcome their instinct for confrontation. Neither was in the domain of the other. The canyon of the Spring of Life was a sacred place; it belonged to all the people. And it had been defiled.

The two Shades stood together, looking at the bloody aftermath of the Seedlings' Ritual of Transformation. Each felt the other's pain. Each sensed the other's fury. The Seedlings had attacked in force. T'mal knew that the people had stood no chance against them. They had been unprepared for the telepathic onslaught of the Seedlings and they did not know how to fight together.

They would have to learn.

Each of them carried a fieldpak and a rifle. They had not known how far it would be necessary to travel until they ran across a Shade, since all Shades in the vicinity of the base had withdrawn from their domains because of previous field excursions, so they had taken enough supplies to last them a week. Paul had not understood why they couldn't simply have taken the shuttle and flown a distance away from the base, where there would be Shades. Certainly landing the shuttle would have posed no problem, since it could easily burn out a clearing for itself.

"That's exactly the problem," Fannon had told him. "Imagine being a Shade and seeing some strange and terrifying metal bird setting down on your domain, belching fire and burning up your foliage. Not exactly the first impression we'd like to make. Besides, we want to try to find a Shade as close to the base as possible. If we can communicate, then we'll try to persuade it to return with us. It'll be easier to get a Shade to come back with us if it won't have to travel too far from its domain. Also, I'd rather try to persuade a Shade to take a walk with us than try talking one into flying on a shuttle. We'll be asking enough as it is."

Paul was glad to see that Fannon was in good spirits. Part of that, perhaps, was due to Shelby, although he wasn't certain. Since Nils had tumbled to the fact that she was capable of projecting, she had been wary of alerting anyone else to the fact, especially Fannon. What was important was that Fannon was in his element. He had taken charge of the expedition, and he was clearly enjoying being away from the base. You couldn't take a man like Fannon, assign him to an established research installation, and expect him to be happy. He was the type of man who needed a challenge. He had to be out in the wild. Jake had said it—"They don't make 'em like Fannon anymore." The moment they had passed the Sturmann field and entered the heavy brush, Fannon had come alive.

Paul himself was thrilled at being allowed to come along. He had requested it, fearing that they would deny him. After all, he was not trained for fieldwork, but Jake had spoken to Fannon and Fannon had agreed to his being included, which surprised him. Paul knew that he was certainly not one of Fannon's favorite people.

"Just stick close to Jake and Nils and don't get underfoot, that's all I ask," Fannon had told him. "And if we run into anything, don't fire unless you're told to. I don't want you hitting anybody in the party."

They walked single-file through the heavy brush, cutting their way through where they had to, but most of the time they were able to pick a path through the thick foliage. Fannon and Shelby were at the head, and Mose Solaway brought up the rear.

It was the first time he had been away from the base, the first time, in fact, that he was experiencing anything remotely like a field excursion. It was one thing, Paul realized, to sit at ColCom HQ and go over mission reports and view record tapes, and it was something else entirely to actually participate. He felt tremendously excited.

The moment they had gone beyond the base perimeter, it felt as if they had entered another world. Paul smiled at the thought. *Of course* it was another world! In the time that he had been at Boomerang Base, he had grown accustomed to the manicured look of the compound, to being surrounded by buildings and people, to being protected. He had said that the people of the base had become isolated from their environment, and only now was he able to appreciate just how true that was.

Tall, slender trees rose high over their heads, blocking off the sun. Shafts of light penetrated here and there through their leafy boughs, making the moisture glisten on the large fronds of the plants that grew at ground level, some of them as tall as Paul was, some taller. On some of the tree trunks, Paul saw brown-and-green-mottled beetles clustered in bunches. The smallest of them were as large as his fist, and they looked like scarabs with mandibles measuring several inches long. He had looked apprehensively at these until Nils had noticed and, laughing, plucked one off a tree. He held it in the palm of his hand and Paul watched nervously as it crawled up his arm, its mandibles gently testing the unfamiliar surface. Its movements were ponderously sluggish.

"They're not interested in us," Nils said. "They feed on the outermost layer of bark which some of these trees shed as a snake sheds its skin. Similar, in fact, to palm trees back on Earth. We call them tree turtles, but you're right to be cautious. Not all the creatures here are quite this friendly."

He gently plucked the beetle off his arm and placed it back on the tree trunk.

From time to time, Paul would see the large, gawky-looking golden birds that he had seen flying in flocks over the base. They nested high up in the trees in large, basket-shaped nests made of small branches and vines that seemed cleverly interwoven. In flight, they were astonishingly graceful and lovely to watch. Hopping among the upper branches, they seemed ungainly, and they greeted the humans with a show of aristocratic indifference.

At the end of the first day, they came to a river, and Fannon decided that they would camp upon its bank and cross it in the morning. As they were setting up camp, Nils pointed out some large, spreading bushlike trees upon which grew in profusion light-green globes the size of oranges.

"Those you want to be very careful of," he said. "See those round, large nutlike things? Those are seedpods."

"Like those the Shades use in their catapults?" said Paul.

"Exactly. You see those strange little trees growing by the water, with the curved trunks and the leaves growing on the sunward side?"

"That's what they make their catapults from?"

"Mmm-hmm. I'm glad you've been doing your homework.

107

They find trees like that, their trunks, actually, which dried out and fell into the water. The water smooths them out and they do the rest with stone knives. They fashion them into paddle-shaped slings and then, very carefully, they pick seed-pods from those nutfruit trees. They have to get them just right, so that they're ready to burst but aren't too fragile. When they fall to the ground, the seedpots burst, sending out a cloud of spores. Inhaling them will drop a hellhound on the spot, and they're just as lethal to us, so it wouldn't do to brush against those branches, if you know what I mean."

"I'll keep that in mind. Are there any other plants you can think of which I should beware? Carnivorous ferns or strangler vines or some such?"

Nils laughed. "Nothing quite that dramatic. At least, nothing that we've run across yet. Our cataloguing of the Boomerang flora and fauna is fairly extensive, but there are bound to be forms of plant and animal life we don't know about yet. You've had an opportunity to study the hazards file?"

He had. He had made a point of it before leaving on the mission. He had known that the seedpods were dangerous, but he was just as glad that Nils had stressed the fact and pointed them out to him. It was one thing to view a computer graphic and another to see the real thing. It made the potential threat more immediate. The hazards file, as its name suggested, extracted from the general computer catalog all the things on Boomerang which were hazardous or potentially hazardous to humans. It was only necessary to vocally request the information and a lightning-quick file search followed, after which the output could be received either vocally, on the screen, or in a printout. Paul had elected to view the information on the monitor.

First on the list, which went without saying, were the hellhounds. There was a tape of hellhounds available, as well. Altogether, the list of hazards was nowhere near as extensive as Paul would have expected. There were ten varieties of insect life to be wary of, from the flitterbirds, which were not technically birds at all but a large species of stinging moth, to the yak beetles, large, football-sized bugs covered with a thick and stringy pelt rather than a chitinous shell. They were especially hard to spot on the tree bark. They were not attracted to humans for any reason, but contact with their hairy pelts could produce anything from a burn to a painful swelling, since they excreted a toxic oil that was a severe irritant to human skin. The sting of a flitterbird, on the other hand, depending upon the individual's reaction, could either result in fever and severe bouts of vomiting or death. The list of plant hazards was somewhat more extensive, containing twenty-six varieties. Of these, most were potentially hazardous only if taken internally. The seedpods were number one on this list, followed closely by the fireapples. These were fruit-bearing trees. The fruit they bore resembled a cross between apples and pomegranates, and they looked temptingly delicious. Shades could eat them without harm, but they produced strong reactions in humans which ranged from a killer case of diarrhea to incapacitating cramps and acute inflammation of the stomach lining. Several varieties of plants were capable of producing rashes and blistering of the skin; others had sharp thorns or husks which could break the skin and raise the risk of infection.

None of the animals, with the exception of the hellhounds, had so far proved to be dangerous, but caution was advised in any case and there was a list of those it was inadvisable to hunt for food. Several species of large birds would attack if provoked or if their nests were threatened, and of these the most dangerous were the condor hawks, so named because of their size and their ferocity. They did not expect to run into these because the condor hawks nested in the mountains. There were snakes on Boomerang and several varieties of reptile life. Ironically, the largest of these, although terrifying to behold, were essentially harmless. There was a slug python; the largest they had seen was as long as its Terran namesake and as thick around as a man's thigh. They left wide, glistening trails, and the only hazard they posed was if one happened to fall on you. There was also a small, rat-faced lizard Fannon called Two-step Charlie, because that was about all you had time for after being bitten.

Among the aquatic life on Boomerang, there were several varieties of river fish that were highly unpalatable and an eel the size of a man's arm that could bestow a painful bite, but that if cooked made a very tasty meal. Fannon had said, with a shudder of distaste, that Shelby ate them raw. Shades did not cook their food. As yet, they knew nothing about what could be found in Boomerang's oceans. A source of major concern were the microorganisms on Boomerang. Tremendous advances had been made in immunocompetent research, but there were still major risks involved in introducing humans into an alien environment. Boomerang Base had seen one virus epidemic shortly before Paul's arrival. Fortunately, there had been no fatalities and they had developed a serum to combat it. All in all, the human body had proved easily adaptable to life on Boomerang. Still, there was much they did not know yet and strict caution was advised in the field. Mercifully, as Nils had pointed out, Boomerang had nothing even vaguely similar to a mosquito. They could camp safely on the riverbank.

They found a small clearing and erected their nysteel mesh tents, which would keep them dry in case of rain and were virtually impregnable while retaining great flexibility. Fannon set up their perimeter defense system, which consisted of several independent tracking systems mounted on small metal bases which he assembled quickly and easily. Each system consisted of a black box with an adjustable tracking turret that was motion-sensitive. They could have opted for a smaller version of the Sturmann field, but Fannon explained that it was impractical, since it would have added a great deal of weight to what they already had to carry, besides which, it would have necessitated clearing away any trees with overhanging branches from which an animal could leap down into the camp, thereby bypassing the field. Such a task would have taken an inordinate amount of time and effort and there was no point to it, since they would be spending only one night in their location. The motion-sensitive laser tracking system was far more efficient for the job. A number of such units could be set up around the camp, adjusted for degree of motion and size of the intruder. The turrets would swivel all night, at preset sweeps, and if they picked up an intruder, the sensing unit would begin to emit a steady series of beeps while at the same time a low-intensity laser would be activated, providing a line-of-sight indication of the location of the intruder. The system could be set to fire a stun charge from a second turret, linked to the laser tracking beams, or it could kill. The option Fannon had selected, since he did not wish to harm any life forms unnecessarily, was to simply have the laser turrets track the potential intruder. The beam would give him a constant indication of the intruder's location and he could then use a remote-control unit to either fire at the intruder or cancel the alert.

"We'll be taking turns on watch," he said, showing Paul how to work the remote-control unit. "These things will probably be beeping on and off all night, so don't get panicky. We are out in the brush, after all, and things move around at night. Just make sure of your target before you elect to shoot. If you have any doubts, just call me on your communicator.

It'll be right next to me in my tent. All you need to do is speak softly—I'm a real light sleeper."

As it began to grow dark, they made a fire and sat around it eating their field rations. They listened to the sounds of the night, to the far-off howls of hellhounds pouncing on their prey, the cries of the night birds and the singing of the carpenter beetles, which emitted sounds like the rasping of thousands of tiny saws biting into wood.

Paul was given the first watch. Mose Solaway, Jake, and Fannon had turned in; Nils and Shelby stayed up to keep him company. Nils did not have to go on watch until the early-morning hours and Shelby would be up all night. The Ones Who Were had no need of sleep, so in effect there would be two keeping watch at all times. They sat together in front of the small fire they had made. Nils toyed with a stick, poking at the embers. Paul nervously held the remote-control unit.

"I feel as though I have gone back in time," said Paul.

Nils smiled. "You have."

Paul chuckled. "Oh, I don't mean ghosting back here. I mean that I feel like a modern man trapped in some prehistoric time. I almost expect to see a dinosaur walk into the camp."

"Yes, I know that's what you meant," said Nils. "Fortunately, we have nothing quite so large here."

"You feel at home out here, don't you?" Paul asked Shelby.

She nodded. "It's a strange feeling, in a way," she said. "Before I became merged, the closest thing I ever had to a home was a survey ship. But I have roots here now. The environment out here is as familiar to me as the control room of a ship, or more so. I have a history here."

Several of the sensor units began beeping, and Paul sat up tensely, clutching the remote-control box. Pencil-thin beams of bright-red light stabbed into the forest from several of the defense units. There was a rustling of brush out in the darkness. They heard a low, rumbling growl coming from a short distance beyond the camp perimeter. It sounded like something very large indeed.

"Well, we've attracted the interest of at least one hellhound," Nils said calmly.

Paul nervously licked his lips. "Should I fire?"

"Relax," said Nils. "You'll have plenty of time. All you have to do is push a button—the unit can't miss. The fire will most likely keep anything away."

111

One of the red beams swept back and forth; the two others indicating points beyond the perimeter stayed still.

"That's the hound," said Nils, pointing at the moving beam. "It's pacing back and forth out there, trying to make up its mind what to do about us. The others are probably some smaller creatures that were attracted by the light, and now they're frozen stiff, hoping that the hound won't notice them."

The beam tracking the hound stopped suddenly, then abruptly swept sharply across toward one of the other beams. The two other beams, which had been motionless seconds ago, suddenly jerked sharply, tracking the animals as they bolted. The hound's beam, moving with astonishing swiftness, intersected one of the others, and the two beams seemed to vibrate, dancing up and down and to the sides. The third beam winked out as one of the animals fled out of range. There was the sound of thrashing out beyond the perimeter, and then only one of the beams remained on. They heard the slathering, crunching sounds of the hellhound feeding on whatever it was that it had caught.

"Law of the jungle," Nils said softly.

Paul glanced at Shelby and saw her violet eyes, like those of a cat, glowing in the dim firelight. She looked like a predatory beast.

# CHAPTER ELEVEN

They were all awake by sunrise. It didn't take long for them to break up camp following an early breakfast, just after first light. During the night, on several occasions, hellhounds had tried to get into the camp and were driven off by the perimeter defense system. In spite of being nervous about the hellhounds, Paul found that he had slept soundly. He was unaccustomed to physical exertion, and the trip was taking a lot out of him. His feet hurt and his muscles were sore. He was grateful when it was time to bed down for the night.

It was maddening to him to see Shelby moving with such ease through the difficult terrain. He kept stumbling and tripping over vines and roots, and his fieldpak seemed after a while to weigh a ton. Shelby moved through the brush as though she were out for a short stroll around the base. The others were all in better shape than he was, and his chief concern was that he didn't slow them down, but even Fannon had to take a back seat to Shelby in the wild. Because of her Ones Who Were, Paul realized, he was seeing her for the first time in her native habitat.

They crossed the river on inflatable nysteel foot pontoons. It was the first time Paul had ever used them. Standing on the riverbank, he watched Nils and Fannon step out onto the water, moving languidly, gliding forward easily on the pontoons by shifting their weight slightly and "sliding" their feet. On the ground, the devices seemed exceedingly cumbersome, but the moment he got out on the water, they threatened to slip out from under him and he flailed his arms for balance. He found himself starting to turn sideways and drift downstream, and he became alarmed. It was with great difficulty that he was able to retain his balance, his ungainly efforts providing a source of amusement to the party. He was grateful when Shelby glided up beside him and steadied him, guiding him across as they crossed the river on a diagonal, drifting with the current.

During the next couple of days, they ran into more hellhounds. The animals seemed to be ubiquitous, and Paul had ample opportunity to observe their ferocity firsthand. The first encounter happened shortly after they had crossed the river.

They were picking a path through the dense forest when the animal struck. Fannon was up front and Shelby was directly behind Paul. Suddenly, she shoved him forward, and as he stumbled, she swung her rifle up and fired. The beast had dropped down on them from overhead, where it had been lurking in the heavier, lower tree branches. It all happened with incredible speed, and it was over before Paul realized what was happening. The beast fell on Nils, who walked directly in front of Paul, knocking him to the ground. Hearing the discharge of Shelby's rifle, Jake and Fannon quickly spun around, bringing their own weapons to bear, but the hellhound was already dead. Shelby had shot it in midair, a

113

feat that would have been impossible for someone with normal human reflexes.

Seeing the ugly brute up close was a good deal different from viewing tapes of them, Paul realized. He had known that they were large, but he was still unprepared for the size of the beast. It was jet black and sleek, like a panther, only significantly larger. Nils was fortunate to have avoided injury from the fearsome-looking claws the beast possessed. Standing on its hind legs, the hound would have dwarfed him. Paul and Jake bent down to lift the carcass, which had Nils pinned underneath.

"The bastard's heavy," Jake said through gritted teeth as he and Paul struggled to lift it off Nils.

Nils looked up at them with a wan smile. "I've noticed," he said. His voice sounded shaky, not that Paul could blame him.

After they had dragged the hound's carcass off Nils, Paul stood up and took a deep breath.

"If that had happened to me, I think I would have had a coronary," he said, swallowing hard.

"I very nearly did," said Nils, getting to his feet shakily.

Within hours, it happened yet again.

The first hound had struck silently. This one's howling chilled Paul to the bones as it came charging straight at them with blurring speed. Fannon stood his ground and shot it just as it was beginning its leap, and it crumpled to the ground. They pressed on, and Paul stepped around it very carefully. From that point on, his palms sweated and there was an almost constant prickling of the hairs at the back of his neck as he imagined hounds lurking in every tree, concealed in every bush. He was beginning to regret asking to go along on the excursion. He held his rifle at the ready, looking all about him, expecting at any moment to confront a beast leaping at him, jaws agape, claws bared. When they made camp that night, he was certain that he would not get a wink of sleep for fear of terrors real and imagined, but his exertions took their toll and he was sound asleep within moments of lying down inside his tent. He dreamed that he was all alone, running madly through the jungle as hordes of hellhounds pursued him, howling and nipping at his heels. He felt their hot breath upon his neck and screamed. He awoke, not knowing if he had actually screamed or if it had been part of the dream. Fannon stuck his head into his tent.

"You all right?" he said.

"I . . . yes, I suppose, why do you ask?"

"Oh, I heard you moving around in there and thought maybe I should check. Sorry if I woke you up."

"No, quite all right. It must have been a dream."

Perfectly straight-faced, Fannon said, "Yes, it must have been. Go on back to sleep."

Still not certain if he had actually screamed, Paul lay back down, feeling embarrassed. He expected to receive some ribbing the next day, but there was no further mention of it. At breakfast, they discussed their disappointment at not having run into any Shades yet.

"Three days out," said Shelby. "I would have thought we would have seen a Shade by now. Yet I've seen no evidence of recent Shade presence anywhere."

"They've obviously withdrawn farther back from the base than we realized," said Nils. "We're quite a disruptive influence."

"We've only brought enough supplies for a week," said Shelby. "Unless we start to rough it and do a little hunting, we'll have to start back tomorrow or the next day."

"Too bad we didn't think to butcher those hounds we killed," said Jake. "There was enough meat there to last us quite a while."

"True enough," said Nils, "but it would have slowed us down a lot to stop and cut some steaks."

"Couldn't we arrange a shuttle airdrop if necessary?" said Paul.

"We could," said Fannon, "but I was hoping that we wouldn't have to. If there are any Shades in the vicinity, the sight of the shuttle might well scare them off."

"Well, I move that we postpone our decision until tomorrow morning," Nils said. "Let's give it another day."

They all agreed and within a short while were on the move once again. Midway through the day, Paul's legs started to cramp up. He forced himself to keep on going, but by this time the others were aware of his difficulties and had slackened their pace somewhat. He was grateful, but frustrated at his inability to keep up with them. The ultimate indignity came when Mose offered to carry his fieldpak for him and Paul found that he was unable to refuse. The fieldpak had seemed light enough when they had left the base, but since that time it had become an oppressive burden and his shoulders were sore. He cursed himself for not having taken the trouble to exercise, but shucking the fieldpak had provided a welcome relief. It was galling that Mose had no trouble with the added weight; in spite of the fact that Mose was bigger and stronger, Paul still felt that giving him the added burden was unfair.

Still carrying his rifle, Paul tried his best to remain alert and was grateful that the day passed uneventfully. Nothing sprang out at them, and there were no great obstacles in their way. There were also no Shades. When they stopped for the night, everyone's disappointment was obvious. Paul was only too glad to find shelter inside his tent, where he lay down and tried not to think about his aching legs or to feel guilty about the fact that the hardship on him was so obvious that he had not even been asked to take a turn in standing watch.

In the morning, he awoke with a strange smell in his nostrils. He opened his eyes and found himself face to face with a nightmarish apparition. It was an eyeless grotesquerie with fleshy antennae and a repulsive-looking, gelatinous mouth that opened and closed slowly with a soft, liquid sound. He shrieked and recoiled from it, leaping to his feet and dashing outside the tent, where he was greeted with howls of laughter.

Fannon had stood the morning watch, and he had allowed a small slug python to slither into the camp. He had dragged it into Paul's tent and deposited it at his side, where it had snuggled up against him, attracted by his body warmth. He had then roused all the others to wait for Paul's reaction upon awaking. When he had burst forth from his tent, his front covered with slick, gleaming slime, his eyes wild with terror, they all doubled over with laughter.

It happened without warning.

Shelby shouted, "Hold your breath!" and even as she cried out, several seedpod globes came arcing gracefully through the air, landing in their midst and bursting.

Paul felt the wind knocked out of him as Fannon hit him full force with a flying leap, carrying both of them back into Paul's tent to land unceremoniously upon the slimy slug, which felt discommoded and slithered outside, where it promptly expired. Immediately, Paul felt Fannon's hand clamp down over his nose and mouth. He lay still, stunned, unable to breathe.

Moments later, they heard Shelby calling them. Before they went outside, Fannon removed a small filtered facemask from Paul's fieldpak, making him put it on over his nose and mouth. Shelby was already wearing hers, and she handed one to Fannon. The attack had been a hit-and-run. Paul froze at the sight of Nils Björnsen and Mose Solaway stretched out on the ground, dead. Their eyes bulged and on the face of each was a horrible rictus. It was a ghastly sight.

As Paul stared at them, horrified, something Nils had said only a short time ago came unbidden to his mind.

*The law of the jungle.*

The perimeter defense turrets swiveled automatically. They were set to kill. Jake had put in a call to the base for a shuttle to come and pick them up. He mentioned only that there had been "some trouble." No use in upsetting anyone; that would come all too soon. There was no question of going on. The bodies of Nils Björnsen and Mose Solaway were placed in one of the tents until the shuttle arrived.

"They waited until we were vulnerable," said Fannon, "until I had taken down the defense system and we were all grouped together."

"Coincidence," said Jake. "They couldn't have known how the system worked. They just happened to attack when they did. Still, it's crazy. Shades have never shown us any hostility, and they don't group together."

"They do now," Fannon said grimly. "There were at least four of them, and the attack was planned. They must have been watching us."

"I can't understand it," Shelby said. *"Why?"*

"I'm less interested in that now than I am in our getting back alive," said Fannon. "They could and probably will hit us again. We should be safe enough with the perimeter defense operating, but no one removes his mask until we're on that shuttle, understood? And stay alert. I don't want to lose anybody else."

"I still can't believe they're dead," said Paul.

"Welcome to fieldwork, Doctor," Fannon said.

"This changes everything," said Jake. "Poor bastards."

"Can the Ones Who Were shed any light on this, Shelby?" Paul said. "Why would Shades want to attack us?"

She simply shook her head. She was, if anything, more shocked at how things had turned out than any of them.

"God," said Jake, "I just remembered Susan."

"Well, one of us has been trained to deal with human emotions," Fannon said. He looked at Paul. "I guess you're the best qualified to tell her."

"I guess I am."

"I'm sorry, Paul."

Paul shrugged helplessly.

A short while later, they tried again. The assault was an abortive one, thanks to the perimeter defenses. Once again, they did not see the Shades, but the system picked them up as they were closing in on the camp. They came in from all sides, and the system, alarms sounding, began firing automatically for a very brief period, then stopped. All was quiet once again. Jake wanted to go out and check, but Fannon wouldn't hear of it.

"Nobody moves a muscle until that shuttle comes, is that clear?" he said.

Jake nodded.

"God, I'd like a cigarette," said Fannon.

Paul realized that he was gripping his rifle so tightly that his hands were beginning to hurt. When the defense system began firing, he had frozen. The rifle would not have been much use to him in that condition.

Although there were no further attacks, they spent a very tense and uneasy day waiting for the shuttle to arrive. None of them felt much like talking. Paul kept glancing at the tent containing the bodies of Mose and Nils. They're dead, he kept saying to himself, they're dead, they're really dead....

Toward late afternoon, Jake started receiving the approaching shuttle on his communicator. They set up a beacon and the shuttle came in as close as possible, burning out a landing area a short distance from their camp. They broke camp with the perimeter defense system still functioning, waiting only until the last possible moment to take it down. Paul got that job. His mouth was dry as he disassembled the apparatus while Fannon, Jake, and Shelby stood by, ready to repel any assault. The time between his starting the job and reaching the shuttle seemed interminable. It was not until they were safely aboard and airborne that Paul was able to relax at all. His hands were shaking. He had never in his life felt so afraid.

T'mal watched the shuttle taking off with a mixture of fear and confusion. The beings that had escaped into the sky were Ones Who Were Not, of that there was no doubt, but these were different from those he had been fighting. These did more than just cause pain to come from a distance. These creatures were able to kill from a distance, as well. The weapons that they used were unlike anything T'mal had ever seen. Twelve of the people had died the true death in an instant. What manner of creatures were these? They were like the others, yet they were also different. The others did not have such weapons, did not wear such peculiar skins. And they had escaped into the sky!

The surviving members of T'mal's party gathered around him, and he could sense that they were frightened. He had no words of comfort to give them. Indeed, if he had, he would not have been able to say them. They did not communicate beyond certain signs they made to each other. They had gathered together out of fear and from their mutual need. They had to do it to survive.

T'mal was older now than he had been when he first saw the Ones Who Were Not. T'kar was still strong within him, even stronger than he had been at first. T'kar was now Great Father. Several times of Need had passed since the slaughter at the Spring of Life, but T'mal had not gone back.

The first time the Need came upon him again, he had fought against it fiercely. His memory of what had happened at the Spring of Life gave him strength, but he had not been able to fully overcome the mating drive. He had started for the mountains, resisting the impulse every step of the way, but his strength of will was failing him. Then he came upon a young female who was also heading for the place of mating. T'kar had made him realize that his only hope was to take the female then and there.

It went against everything T'mal knew. To mate without the Rituals, to disregard the choosing, it was the way of beasts. And yet, he had to choose. It was either the way of beasts or the true death, because T'mal was certain that the Spring of Life would be attacked again, and better the true death than to merge with such savage creatures. And if the female continued on her way, she would also meet that fate. T'mal chose for himself and he chose for her.

With him was the young male he had met during the last time of Need, following the slaughter. They fell on her together, and she was so stunned that for a moment she went utterly limp, but when she realized what they meant to do, she reacted with fury, and T'mal could sense her outrage. She too felt the Need, but she did not wish to be taken in the way of beasts and she did not understand why they should wish to do so. None of the people had ever attempted such a thing. The journey to the Spring of Life, with all its challenges, had to be undertaken in order to prove worthiness; the people had to gather together; the Rituals had to be observed, and it was for the females to choose.

She had succeeded in fighting free of them, and then she had done something none of the people ever did. She had retrieved the spear that she had dropped and she had faced them, making clear her intention to use the weapon if they

119

persisted in their attempt to force themselves on her. But they were two to one, and although she succeeded in inflicting some wounds upon them, they were able to disarm her and force her to the ground. She fought hard, but in the end, she gave in to the strength of the Need and they both had her.

Afterward, she was angry and confused. They remained with her for several days, not allowing her to leave them, an act she clearly did not understand. And when T'mal felt that it was safe, they took her to the Spring of Life. Though he had known what to expect, the sight of the recent carnage still caused T'mal almost unbearable pain. They walked with her among the torn and bloody bodies of the people, and T'mal found what he had been looking for. They had fought, and before it was all over, they had succeeded in killing some of the Ones Who Were Not. T'mal pointed out their bodies to her and, by signs, made her understand what had happened. Some of the people, very few, had survived the massacre, and they found them, wounded, stunned, and gathered them together.

As time went on, they added to their number. T'mal became their leader. They were a sad lot, with no domain, no customs left to them. They stayed together, hunted together, moved from place to place. And they were learning how to fight the invaders.

The Ones Who Were Not had gathered together in several places on their side of the mountains now. T'mal had found these places, where they made bare the ground and made nests for themselves from trees. They had tried to drive them off, but the invaders were too strong, and many of T'mal's people were killed before T'mal learned that the way to fight the Ones Who Were Not was to attack them when their number was small, to fight like beasts, surprising them and then retreating. Sometimes they succeeded; more often they did not. The invaders had a way of sensing when the people were near, of knowing when the attack would come. Sometimes they could catch them unprepared, but this was rare. They were fierce fighters, and even though T'mal was able to kill some of them, there were always more.

Now there were these new invaders, who wore stranger skins, used weapons far more deadly, and could fly up into the sky. How could they fight against such creatures? They were capable of doing things that the people could not do. Yet they could die. T'mal had seen that. It was the only thing that mattered.

# CHAPTER TWELVE

The funeral for Nils Björnsen and Mose Solaway was a grim occasion. They kept it short. Jake said a few words and then they put them in the ground. Paul stood by with Susan Rivers, who watched the proceedings with a glazed expression. Afterward, she had looked at him and said, "I didn't even get the chance to be his widow," then she walked away.

If Fannon felt any grief, he concealed it well. He watched Nils being buried with a stoic expression, then went forward and finished the job himself. The "inner circle" got no sleep that night. They gathered in the mess hall and sat together over coffee. Sean McEnroe joined them. He was uncharacteristically subdued.

"If only you had been able to communicate with them," he said.

Fannon snorted. "They never gave us a chance. Two of us were dead before we even knew what the hell was happening."

"I mean afterward," said Sean.

*"Afterward?"*

"You did say they attacked once more," said Sean. "If you had linked up with the base, I could have patched it through the computer as we had originally intended."

Fannon stared at him with disbelief. "They killed two of our people and you expected us to sit there trying to talk to them while they tried to finish the job?"

Sean took a deep breath. "I don't mean to be insensitive," he said, "but Mose and Nils were gone. Nothing to be done. But you might have forestalled the second onslaught if you were able to talk to them."

"They would have been in range of the perimeter defense by the time we knew that they were there," said Jake.

121

"You could have turned up your communicators all the way," said Sean. "They certainly have the volume, and I could have broadcast a continuous message—'We mean you no harm,' or something of the sort."

"Sure," said Fannon. "And how were we to know that your message would have made them friendly? How were we to know that it would even be understood? We'd have had to let them get inside the perimeter defense in order to find that out, and I was not about to let that happen, not with two men dead."

"Your point is well taken," said Sean, "but the fact that a group of Shades were able to mount what appears to have been an organized assault upon your camp indicates something very significant. In order to interact in such a fashion, they must have developed some manner of communication among themselves, some sort of sign language, undoubtedly. Leave aside, for the moment, the singular significance of that development. The point is, had you been able to capture even one of them and establish communication, you might have gotten through to the others."

"And how were we supposed to do that?" Fannon said wryly.

"Well, for one thing, I don't think it was necessary to set the perimeter defense to kill," Sean said.

"I see," said Fannon. "We were just supposed to stun them and then send someone out, like Jake, perhaps, to pick out a likely-looking prospect and drag him back to camp, is that it?"

"What Drew is saying, Sean," said Shelby, "is that it would have been too dangerous. Jake wanted to go out and check after the second assault, but Drew wouldn't even hear of it. It's quite possible that one or more of the Shades were lying out there, only wounded, but sending anyone out past the perimeter would have been exposing him to attack. It simply wasn't safe."

"Perhaps," said Sean. "Yet the fact remains that whatever the reason for the attack was, you've only reinforced it through your actions. Setting the perimeter defense turrets to stun would have repelled the attack just as effectively."

"For Christ's sake, Sean, they killed Mose and Nils!"

McEnroe stared steadily at Fannon. They were all suddenly silent.

Fannon expelled his breath softly. "Shit," he muttered.

Shelby reached out to touch his shoulder. "Drew . . ."

He shrugged her hand away.

122

"I'm sorry," said Sean.

"So much for holier than thou," said Fannon. "I'm just like they are."

There wasn't a person in the room who did not know that by "they," Fannon meant the people who had sent them to Boomerang.

"If I may interject a comment," said Paul, "I don't think you should blame yourself. When that second attack occurred and the system started firing, I found myself devoutly hoping that it would kill the Shades before they all killed us. I was terrified. The thought of simply stunning them did not even occur to me, and I knew how the system worked. All that I could think of was that I was scared out of my wits and that Nils and Mose were dead. It's difficult, to say the least, to maintain a sense of perspective under such circumstances."

"Thank you, Doctor," Fannon said sarcastically. "That makes a very convenient rationalization. Only I've been there before, remember?"

"You mean Rhiannon."

"Yes, I mean Rhiannon, dammit!"

"It's hardly the same thing," said Paul.

"No, it's not, is it? On Rhiannon, they wiped out practically the whole team. I wasn't thinking about retribution then, and I had a whole lot more reason."

Paul licked his lips nervously. "It isn't the best time to get into this," he said, "but I think perhaps we should get it out into the open. You're an unusual man in many ways. Control is very important to you. You set high standards of conduct for yourself and you possess a high degree of idealism. That enabled you to handle the situation on Rhiannon, in spite of what must have been unbelievable stress."

"Get to the point," said Fannon.

"I was getting to it. Boomerang *is* different. Very different. You don't feel in control here, and that bothers you a great deal. And, subconsciously, you have a strong resentment for the Shades—perhaps you even hate them. It's motiva—"

"That's absurd."

"It's motivated," Paul continued, "by several factors. You've always been resentful of your assignment to this project. It was done against your will and you had no control over it. Nor have you any control over your failing relationship with Shelby, if you'll forgive my indiscretion in bringing the matter up, but this is an unusual situation."

"Go ahead," said Fannon. "Say your piece."

"The fact is," said Paul, "that you'd do anything to get

off-planet and be rid of this mission. The fact is, your resentment of the Directorate, whether justified or unjustified, has reached pathological proportions. The fact is that you're in love with Shelby, but you are incapable of including the Ones Who Were in your feelings for her. You feel hindered by them, threatened, imposed upon. You choose to forget that they are part of the reason why you love her, as they are a part of her. You would have been incapable of having such feelings for her before she became merged. What was she then? A profound neurotic, intensely self-contained and maladjusted, unable to enter into even an ordinary social relationship. Yet now she possesses an active, vibrant nature; she is independent, strong, and assertive and can hold her own and better with the rest of us. In many ways, she is our superior in terms of her abilities and the stability of her personality. These are all qualities you find very attractive. Such qualities in a man would strongly dispose you toward friendship and respect, but you find them threatening in a woman. Especially so since she doesn't need you. The fact that she wants you seems to be immaterial. The Ones Who Were fulfill her needs in a way you never could; they are closer to her than you could ever become. They *are* her. You can't accept that. You see them as coming *between* the two of you. It's impossible. Coming from such a base, you'll never resolve your conflict."

He paused. "I'm sorry if this is embarrassing for you, my speaking like this in front of the others, but we're all in this together. What any of us thinks and does affects the others on a very direct, personal level. None of us can afford to be indulgent of our insecurities any longer. We've got to pull together. If you cannot come to terms with your own feelings, I strongly suggest, both for your own good and the good of the base, that you put them aside. You're an officer, Captain Fannon. You have a job to do."

"You finished?" Fannon said.

"I'm finished."

"I've never liked you, Doctor," Fannon said. "I still don't like you. And I'm not accustomed to being dressed down by a glorified bureaucrat. Especially one who pokes his nose into my private affairs. But you've made a strong case for the fact that we can't afford to think about private affairs now, no pun intended. And you're absolutely right. You're right about a lot of things. Maybe that's why I don't like you, I don't know. I don't need you to remind me of where my duty lies."

Paul watched him closely. His body language was strongly

antagonistic. Fannon seemed to be just on the edge of leaping across the table at him. Suddenly, he seemed to relax.

"On the other hand," said Fannon, "maybe I do need someone to remind me. My apologies." He took a deep breath. "Right. Let's get on with it. It's going to be a long night."

It was almost morning when they finally broke up to get at least a little sleep before the next day's work began. Paul lingered behind, not of a mind to go to bed. Shelby sat with him. They were alone in the otherwise empty mess hall.

"I underestimated Fannon," Paul said.

"He's an easy man to underestimate," Shelby said with a smile.

"I fully expected to have a fight on my hands," Paul said. "A verbal one, if nothing else."

"Just between the two of us," said Shelby, "so did I."

"I've never seen anyone switch gears like that before," said Paul. "He took what I said, and it must have been quite unpleasant for him, digested it, dealt with it, and moved right on. I've never seen anything like it. It's ironic in a way, but a crisis was precisely what he desperately needed. He's in his own element now. It's a sin that we had to lose Nils and Mose for it to happen. That attack was a disaster for the project, and ironically, Fannon is a man who thrives on disaster. It all seems somehow unreal. I saw them put into the ground and yet I still expect to have breakfast with them in another couple of hours. It's insane."

"There is insanity among the people."

Paul looked up sharply. "K'itar?"

"The One That Is required rest. K'ural watches, the others hear. The One That Is will remember what is said."

Paul smiled. "I wish to hell I could do that."

"You require rest?"

"Yes, indeed, I do. But I'm not going to take it. I'd just as soon stay up and talk."

"Then we shall listen."

"Do you think tomorrow's flyover will work?" said Paul.

"We do not know. The people know nothing of shuttles. When R'yal was One That Is, before he merged with Shelby and later became part of the Great Hunter, R'yal was perhaps the first of all the people to see a shuttle. It was one of the ship's lighters used by the first survey team. R'yal did not know it was a flying craft. He took it to be a sort of flying beast sent by the All Father to devour the humans, who were

125

thought to be blasphemous, unholy creatures. The humans were seen to enter the 'mouth' of the beast and be devoured, only to be vomited forth again because the beast could not digest them."

K'ural chuckled. "It seems amusing now. It is good to laugh about it. But there is no humor to be found in what has happened. It is beyond all understanding. When the shuttle flies over the land tomorrow, announcing our intentions to the people, they will doubtless be frightened. They will understand the words, but not the action. They may think the craft is some manner of flying beast, taught the language of the people by the All Father. They may think it is an unholy portent. There is no knowing how they will react. There is no doubt that they will be afraid. This is what we all wanted to avoid, but now it must be done. This new development is a source of great distress to us."

"Have the people *ever* gathered together in the past, for any reason, besides the Need?" said Paul.

"Oh, yes. A long, long time ago. It is the dimmest of memories. A racial memory, as you call it. It was in a time that would compare in human history to your primitive days of being hunter-gatherers. We have evolved much since then, but we are still primitive, by human standards."

"So then it's not an unnatural phenomenon," said Paul.

"No more unnatural than if you were to forget the discovery of fire and once again take to the caves," K'ural said.

"Good point," said Paul. "I keep thinking that we must have done something to cause such a radical change in behavior. It's possible that our mere presence here could account for it, of course, since we've taken over territory that was Shade domain, but I can't help thinking that we simply aren't significant enough as a factor, that we haven't been here long enough to have the kind of influence that would affect them so radically.

"When Shelby first became merged and responded to the Need, Nils and Fannon pulled her out of the canyon of the Spring of Life and in doing so attacked the people, firing stun charges into several. Perhaps that was what was responsible."

"Perhaps," K'ural said. "Still, a stun charge does not kill, and the people killed Mose and Nils. They would have killed all of us."

"Maybe they think we're some new kind of beast that can be hunted for food," Paul said.

"That is hardly likely. Humans do not bear even the most remote resemblance to any beast known by the people. They

126

*do* bear a close resemblance to the people. It can be seen by their behavior that they are not beasts."

"Would that we were so perceptive from the first," said Paul. "There *has* to be some explanation."

"We will not find it here."

"I'm afraid you're right. One thing is certain, and that's that if we can't find the answer to this soon, the Directorate will have to pull us out."

"That is what many of the people here wish."

"I know. What I'm worried about is what the Directorate will do."

They began the overflights early in the morning. The idea had been Fannon's and, after some debate, it had been accepted. There were to be no more field excursions off base, not even short ones in the vicinity of the grounds. There was no reported Shade presence anywhere in the vicinity of the base, but no chances would be taken. No one was to leave, no one was to venture anywhere near the base perimeter, since it was possible that Shades could lob the deadly seed-pods over the Sturmann field and onto the grounds. The shuttle, equipped with a powerful public-address system, would fly continuous missions over half the continent, returning only to refuel and for a change of crew. It would broadcast a continuous message to the Shades in their own language.

The content of that message was hotly debated during the previous night. It was finally decided that no reference to the All Father would be made. It was also decided against telling the Shades that they had come from off-planet, a concept that Shelby had argued would be difficult for them to grasp. Any attempt at explaining the shuttle to them in the message was also decided against, discarded as being too awkward and taking up too much time. The message was kept simple.

"We're going to tell them that we come in peace," said Jake to the assembled personnel at first mess. "We come in peace and we want to meet in friendship. We are people, too. And we'll give them the location of the base. As simple as that. Then we wait and see if they'll come to us."

"Suppose *they* don't come in friendship?" said Susan Rivers, attempting to keep her tone carefully neutral and not quite succeeding.

"That's why we want them to come to us," said Jake. "They can't hurt us here; we're well protected. What's more, we can control their entrance into the compound. Out in the field, any party would be easily exposed to an attack by superior numbers. We'll hold out the olive branch and wait."

"For how long?" asked someone in the crowd.

"As long as necessary," said Jake.

"What if they don't respond?" asked someone else.

"The *Wanderer* will be departing for Gamma 127 soon," said Jake. "Paul Tabarde has persuaded me to move up our departure date. If, within a reasonable period of time, we get no reaction to our message, I will be reporting to the Directorate and recommending that this project be terminated, because of extreme hazard to the personnel."

That remark prompted an undertone of conversation that began to grow in volume until Jake rapped upon the table several times to restore silence.

"I know a lot of you want to go home," said Jake. Then, after a pause, "Whatever you regard as being home. I know that many of you have expressed a desire not only to leave Boomerang, but to leave the service, as well."

This time, when he paused, the silence was a palpable one.

"You should know that may not be possible," said Jake. "I caution you not to have any expectations whatsoever. Our situation here has changed dramatically. All we can do is ride it out and see what happens."

"If you ask me, I think it's a waste of time," said Andrew Brock.

He flew the shuttle low over the treetops at minimal speed, the message repeating over and over again on the public-address system.

"You don't think it's going to work?" said Leila Bascomb. She was charting their course so that succeeding flight crews would not duplicate their efforts.

"I doubt it," Andrew said.

"Why?"

"I keep trying to put myself in their place," said Andrew. "I mean, look, how would you feel if some alien race set down on Earth without asking anyone's permission, drove off a segment of the population in the landing area, and set about building a small city?"

"We didn't *drive* them off," said Leila.

"It amounts to the same thing."

"What brought this on?" she said.

"How did you feel when you found out about Mose and Nils?" he countered.

She was silent for a moment. "Shocked," she said at last. "Sad for Susan. Frightened."

"You didn't feel angry?"

"Of course I felt angry."

He nodded. "So did I. I found myself wishing that I had been there with them, so I could have done something. Struck back. It really turned me around."

"I think most of us felt the same way," she said.

"The thing is," said Andrew, "we've underestimated the Shades."

"How so?"

"We haven't had any respect for them, and we should have known better. We know a lot more about them than they know about us, thanks to Shelby, but we still regarded them as some sort of docile, simple primitives. It's happened time and again throughout history, when people with superior technology ran across more primitive races. Hi, guys, here we are with our civilization. Isn't it wonderful? Well, we're going to make you a present of it. And no one ever stops to think that they might not want it. We've pushed them too far and now they're fighting back. Hell, they're only defending themselves."

"So what's the solution?" she said.

"I think we should just pack up and get the hell out," said Andrew. "Leave them alone. They don't want us here."

"I can understand that," Leila said, "but we don't exactly have a choice, do we?"

"What we—what the *hell*?"

"What is it?"

"See for yourself."

They were approaching an area in the forest that had been cleared. And what they were seeing was a village.

"But I thought Shades didn't construct shelters!" Leila said.

"Yeah, and they don't group together and attack people, either," said Andrew. "Get on the horn to the base. I'm going in for a closer look."

As Leila contacted the base, Andrew Brock took the shuttle in low around the edge of the village, circumscribing it.

"Leila, those aren't Shades!"

"*Repeat that,*" said the base control.

"Those look like *people* down there," said Brock. "They look human!"

"*What?*"

"The residents of the village appear to be human," said Brock. "Primitives, but human! They're waving us down!"

*"Leila, has he gone crazy?"*

"It's true," she said in an astonished voice. "I can't believe it!"

"I'm taking her down."

*"Negative, Brock."*

"But—"

*"Repeat, negative. Under no circumstances are you to land. Take a pass over the village and give us a transmission."*

"Will do."

Moments later, Jake Thorsen came on.

*"Brock? Get back here on the double."*

"Don't you want me to—"

*"Now!"*

"Yes, sir."

They replayed the transmission from the shuttle. They saw a village of wood cabins, arranged in the style of a fortified camp, with a wooden wall around the village. There were several wells, what seemed to be a larger main building, some smaller structures, and several guard towers. It was a place built to be well defended from assault.

The people certainly looked human. They were dressed in leather clothing made from animal skins, and they all wore their hair long, although some braided it and others gathered it together to be tied at the back of the neck. At the sight of the shuttle, they displayed a great deal of excitement. Many more of them ran out into the open, pointing and gesturing. They did not appear to be at all afraid. And, judging by their gestures, they had indeed wanted the shuttle to land.

The screen went blank.

"Well, what do you make of that?" said Jake.

"That village wasn't there before," said Fannon.

"Before what?"

"We mapped out that area pretty well during the first survey mission," Fannon said. "There was nothing there."

"It does look like a recent construction," said Jake.

"I never saw those people before," said Fannon. "Where the hell did they come from?"

"We never did explore beyond the mountains," Shelby said. "Perhaps they're a mutation of the Shades that we've never seen before?"

"Have the Ones Who Were ever seen them?"

"No."

"Somehow I didn't think so."

"You think they're human, Drew?"

"They sure look human, don't they?"

"Suppose they are."

"Where did they come from? Why are they living like that? Why didn't we know anything about them? No ship has arrived since we've come, nothing."

"Suppose they're not human?" said Jake.

"Then I would think that it was a bit too much of a coincidence that they look so much like us," said Fannon.

"They did appear to be reacting to the broadcast message," said Paul.

"Perhaps," said Sean McEnroe. "On the other hand, the message might have meant nothing to them. Maybe they were reacting only to the sight of the shuttle. What matters is we now have an answer to why Mose and Nils were killed. The construction of that village clearly indicates a conscious plan to defend against attack. And *organized* attack, at that. Whether they are human or not, they look like us. The Shades attacked one of our parties, killed two of our people. It was never us that the Shades intended to attack. It was *them*."

Shelby sat silently, trying to follow the discussion and at the same time come to terms with the tremendous confusion in her mind. The Ones Who Were had never seen the people gather together in order to fight against humans or creatures who resembled humans. It simply made no sense. They had lived out countless lives without ever seeing anything remotely like it.

"Let's not try to be too clever," said Paul, "or we'll wind up outsmarting ourselves. Certain things we're never going to know for sure until we investigate, but counting ten before we go rushing into anything is a good idea. All right, so they appear to be human. And there has never before been any evidence of intelligent beings who resemble humans so closely as to be indistinguishable from the standpoint of at least a superficial examination such as we have here, not on Boomerang, not anywhere. We've had humanoids, but never anything *that* close. The Shades are the closest beings to humans in appearance that we've found to date. My inclination is to proceed on the assumption that a rose is a rose because it looks like one, at least until I've had proof to the contrary."

131

"So if they're human, again, where in hell did they *come* from?" Fannon said.

"One possible explanation occurs to me right now," said Paul. "Jake, ships have been lost in the process of ghosting, right? There has never been any explanation as to what happened to those ships. Perhaps we've finally found one. Wouldn't it be possible, through some sort of accident involving Zone travel, for a ship to have become lost and to have arrived here?"

"What would have stopped them from simply going back the way they came once their error was discovered?" Fannon said.

"He may have something there, Fannon," Jake said. "There *is* one thing that would have stopped them, and that is if they somehow managed to go back far enough in time, before the Zone technology was in existence. That wouldn't be too difficult, theoretically. After all, *you* predate Zone travel. If something like that happened, they couldn't turn around and go back. There would be no departure points, no Hansen magnets, no Twilight Zone. They'd be trapped."

"You're saying that these people are the descendants of our hypothetical . . . what? Zone castaways?"

"It would make sense," said Jake. "It would explain why they didn't panic when they saw the shuttle. They'll be thinking that rescue is at hand."

"I don't know," said Sean. "On the one hand, if they've been here for a significant period of time, it could explain the altered behavior in the Shades. Maybe. I don't know. If we accept this hypothesis, then the reason why they were never seen by the first survey could be that they're nomadic. As Jake said, the village appears to be a recent construction. None of the cabins are really weathered. But if they've been here that long, what about degeneration? And where is their ship? They surely would not have tried to *land* it, but the *Wanderer* is the only ship in orbit."

"Perhaps something happened to their ship," said Paul.

"Short of its blowing up, I can't think of anything that could have happened to it that would not have left at least *some* traces," Sean said.

"Maybe that's what happened."

"Well, now that's fucking absurd, Paul," said Sean. "Ships don't just happen to blow up, not unless you want them to. And *that* would be positively insane. If you were marooned on some planet, would you destroy your only means of es-

132

cape? To say nothing of the fact that a better signal beacon than a ship in a parking orbit simply does not exist."

"How about this?" said Paul. "They realized that they couldn't get back, so they established a primitive sort of base on Boomerang while the ship went on an exploratory flight, to see if there wasn't a more hospitable planet within reach. Something happened and the ship did not return."

"How about we *ask* them?" Fannon said.

"But what if they *aren't* human?" Jake said.

"Either way, it should prove interesting," said Sean.

"The village is very primitive, from what I've seen," said Paul. "I rather doubt they would have anything in the way of weaponry which could pose a serious threat."

"That's how we felt about the Shades, remember?" Jake said. "Still, they caught us by surprise. Perhaps we're being a bit too paranoid."

"When you're in the field, there's no such thing as being too paranoid," said Fannon. "And a rock would be a serious threat if you got brained with it, as Goliath discovered. However, the point is that we're not going to accomplish anything by sitting here and playing guessing games. Sometimes you have to take a risk and sometimes people die. It's tough, but that's fieldwork. It's what you wanted, Jake, and now you've got it. We've got to make a decision about this. I think there's something very strange happening here, and we're not going to find out what it is unless we go and pay a call on our new neighbors."

"I think he's right," said Shelby, "but I'm going to stay behind here, and I'd like Sean to remain with me, in case any Shades should respond to our broadcast."

"All right," said Jake. "In that case, we'll take the shuttle out. It should afford us adequate protection. Fannon, you'll come, of course, and Paul, I'd like you along, as well. We'll take Brock and Bascomb with us—they'll remain with the shuttle—and Shelby, you make sure there's someone on duty receiving us around the clock, okay?"

"Right."

"We'll be checking in at least once every hour," said Jake. "If we fail to make a check in, you send someone out to get us."

They were loading up the shuttle when the Shades came.

# CHAPTER THIRTEEN

T'mal could not see the wall, but he could *feel* it. He had started to walk forward toward the strange new village when one of the others pulled him back. It had been the one who had led them to this place. This one's domain had once been close by. T'mal had not understood until the one who had restrained him motioned him to wait. Then he had watched while a branch was torn from a nearby tree and thrown toward the village. It had made no sense to him, there seemed to be no purpose in the act, but then he saw the branch *hurled back*, as if it had struck something. Only there had been nothing there. There had been a sharp popping sound and the branch bounced back, as though changing direction of its own accord. Several of the people drew back in frightened confusion.

T'mal bent down and picked up the branch. It did not look any different. Holding it out before him, T'mal slowly advanced. When he was almost to the point where the branch had bounced back from seemingly empty air, he carefully stretched the branch forward. Once again, he heard the popping sound and the branch tried to wrench itself out of his hand. He repeated the action with the same results. Then, tentatively, he stretched out just his hand. Slowly . . . very slowly . . .

Simultaneously, T'mal heard the popping sound and his hand recoiled. He snatched it back, holding his wrist with his other hand. There was a tingling, burning sensation, a brief and incandescent pain, but his hand seemed unharmed.

"There is great power here," said Great Father T'kar.

"The others have no such power," said T'mal.

"Or we have not seen it," said K'dan, the Great Hunter.

"No," said T'mal, "they have no such power. If they had,

134

they would have used it. These beings are different somehow. They are the same, and yet they are different."

"Their offer of friendship is false," said Great Mother N'tari. "They mean the people harm."

"With such power as they have, they could have already harmed the people," said T'mal. "They could have fallen on us from the sky in their flying beast."

"This is true," T'kar said. "This beast which is not a beast is a fearsome thing. And it spoke in our tongue. We have come to listen. If these beings wish to fight, then we will fight. But first we will listen."

"We will wait until they come," T'mal said.

"How many of them are there?" said Jake.

"Can't say," Shelby replied. "I count at least twenty, but there may be more just out of sight."

"Well, congratulations, Sean," said Jake. "Looks like you've broken through to them."

"That still remains to be seen," said Sean. "What's our next move?"

"Letting them all inside the camp is out of the question," said Jake. "Maybe we can convince just one of them to come inside while the others wait."

"I somehow get the feeling that's not going to be easy," Fannon said. "Just the same, Jake, I agree with you. Sean, get on that computer. Shelby, with all due respect, I'd like you to stay back from this one. It must have taken them a lot just to come here; one look at you and there's no telling how they might react. Okay?"

She nodded, but she didn't look happy about it. "I'll go with Sean," she said.

"Right," said Jake. "Let's go see if we can't start a conversation. Let's move forward slowly."

They moved out toward the perimeter, approaching the Shades slowly and deliberately. The Shades stood fast, but they looked tense. It was the first time Paul had ever seen Shades in the flesh. He couldn't take his eyes off them.

Shelby Michaels had an arresting appearance, because of her mutation, but these beings were *all* Shade, and they were striking, indeed. Their skin was a pale-gray color and their manes were thick, shaggy, and starkly white. Their eyes were a deep violet, and they glowed with a light of their own, like cats' eyes. Their resemblance to humans was startling. The features, except for the eyes, were identical. The Shades possessed three fingers with an opposed thumb, each finger

135

proportionately heavier and stronger than that of a human. They would have a very powerful grip. Their chests looked strangely different. Paul knew this was due to the greater number of ribs that Shades possessed. There were thirty-two of them, thinner and more flexible than human ribs, linked by a correspondingly stronger system of cartilaginous tissue. Their hearts were in the exact center of their chests, and their lungs had a much greater capacity than human lungs. The smallest of the Shades was well over seven feet tall. Humans were bulkier and possessed greater muscle density, but the Shades still would have the strength advantage because of their longer bones and greater flexibility.

Looking at them, Paul found it hard to believe that these strangely beautiful beings would be perceived as beasts back on Earth and in the colonies. They looked more like humans than any other known form of life. Yet, Paul remembered bitterly, it wasn't all that long ago, historically speaking, that blacks were regarded as inferior. There was no logic to prejudice.

They stopped within a short distance of the Shades, separated from them by the invisible Sturmann field. The bodies of the Shades were tense and there was an alertness in their manner. They all seemed to be staring intently at him.

"Why are they looking at me like that?" said Paul.

Fannon glanced at him and made a wry face. "Because you're black," he said. "Stupid of me. I asked Shelby to remain behind because I was concerned that her appearance might confuse them, but I didn't even think about you."

Paul smiled. "Strangely enough, I suspect there might be a sort of compliment in there somewhere. Or something."

He was not the only black among the personnel. There were several others of mixed ancestry ranging from African to his Creole. There were also people of East Asian, South American, and Amerindian descent. The Shades were all uniformly gray. Obviously, they had seen humans before, but just as obviously, the idea of humans possessing differing racial characteristics was one for which they had no reference.

Moving very slowly and deliberately, Jake produced his communicator. Paul saw the fingers of the Shade nearest to him tighten around the shaft of its spear.

"Well, here goes," said Jake. "Sean, you reading me?"

*"Loud and clear, Jake."*

"Now that I'm here, I'm not sure what to say," said Jake.

*"Why don't you let Shelby and me handle it from here?"*

"Okay, but let me know what you're telling them."

*"Right. First we'll tell them that we mean no harm, that we've come in peace and that we'd like to speak to them so that we may be able to understand each other."*

"Fire when ready."

Jake turned up the volume on his communicator slightly, and within seconds, the language of the Shades began to come from the communicator as Sean instructed the computer to program the synthesizer to make the appropriate sounds. Paul found that the language of the Shades made him think of a combination of guttural, Semitic speech extremely modified by electronics and some of the sawtooth wave harmonics popularized by the avant-garde composers of the early nineties. It was a bizarre sound that he did not find very pleasant to the ear, but it had an electrifying effect upon the Shades.

*"How's it going?"* Sean said.

"They understood it, all right," said Jake. "Unfortunately, they can't talk back to us."

*"Well, I think I can fix that, provided they're willing to give us some cooperation,"* Sean said. *"But I'm going to need at least one of them in the lab."*

"Good luck. Well, go ahead and tell them."

Paul watched as they listened to the next frenetic burst of Shade speech. Then he watched a startling piece of mime. One of the Shades drew a straight line in the dirt with its spear. Then it approached the line and jerked, as if stung by some insect.

"The field," Fannon said. "Okay. Let's show 'em." He took a nullifier out of his pocket. Then he faced Paul and held both hands out in front of him, palms out, motioning at Paul. "Paul, move back several steps. Right, a little more. Okay."

He then faced the Shades and made the same motions. They understood and backed off a short distance. Fannon turned off the section of the field between the two Sturmann poles to their left and right. He worked the nullifier so that the Shades could clearly see what he was doing. Then, slowly and deliberately, he crossed the plane where the field had been and then went back again. He motioned the Shades forward. They all moved forward together, slowly. Fannon immediately made the same backing-off motions. They stopped and backed off, watching him intently.

"Sean, tell them only one," he said.

The message was relayed. The Shades exchanged glances, miming to each other and pulling at each other. One of the

137

Shades, clearly the leader, stopped them. He took one of the other Shades by the arm and pulled him alongside. They both took two steps forward and stopped.

"Not one, but two," said Fannon.

"We can handle two," said Jake. "Sean, tell them it's okay with us."

Another burst of speech came from the communicator. This time, the head Shade drew a line in the dirt once more and crossed it with the other Shade by his side. The moment they crossed their dirt line, the Shade took its spear and turned it around, miming its being thrust into his own abdomen.

"What the . . .?"

"How do we know you won't kill us once we cross the line?" Paul said.

"Jackpot," said Fannon. "You just earned your day's pay, Doc."

"Only how are we going to convince them?" Jake said.

"We give them hostages," said Fannon.

"That would be taking one hell of a chance," said Jake.

"We're paid to take chances," Fannon said. "Besides, look at it from their point of view."

"I'll go," said Paul. "I came here to study their behavior, after all. I'm not going to get a better chance."

Fannon nodded. "Okay, Doc. You and me. Sean, explain it to them."

As the communicator "spoke" once more, Fannon and Paul stepped forward together. The leader of the Shades pointed to Paul and imitated Fannon's back-off motions. Then he pointed at Jake.

"I get it," Paul said. "I'm not good enough, eh?"

Fannon chuckled. "Don't be so touchy, Doc. I think I get it. Their leader's going to come with us, so they want to be sure to get *our* leader. Seems they've figured out that Jake is it."

"It does seem only fair, doesn't it?" said Jake. "Okay. We'll do it their way. Sean?"

*"Still here."*

"Fannon and I are going to be the hostages. Pull everybody back out of the way. I don't want the Shades to see any of our people between here and the lab. I want a clear road. I don't want anything to provoke them or make them any more nervous than they are."

*"You got it."*

Jake nodded and took a deep breath. "Right. Let's get on

138

with it. I suppose we'd better give them some idea of when they can expect their people back."

*"How about sunrise tomorrow?"* Sean said. *"I need some time with them. Think you can rough it for one night?"*

"I'm not wild about it, but I suppose it'll have to do," said Jake. "Just don't be late, okay?"

Sean relayed the message to the Shades. The leader and the second Shade stepped forward. Both pairs slowly crossed the line at the same time. Jake and Fannon disappeared into the forest with the other Shades. Paul reactivated the field and turned to the two Shades standing before him. Both held their weapons at the ready.

"I'm just as nervous as you are," Paul said. He pointed out the way to the Shades. They motioned with their spears. "After me, huh?" He swallowed hard, not at all happy about the idea of two spears at his back. Then he turned and began to walk purposefully toward the lab, where Sean waited with Shelby. He did not look back. The Shades followed.

T'mal watched carefully as they followed the dark human, but they did not see any others. The land that these creatures had claimed for their domain had been much changed. He marveled at the strange structures all around him. He had seen the other humans building their structures in their villages, so he knew how those were made, but these were a mystery. As they were entering one of these structures, T'mal hesitated, cautiously feeling the strange material with his hand. He did not know what it was. It felt smooth and cold. It could not have been made from any living thing. Inside the structure, there was light. This amazed T'mal. It was as though they had taken pieces of the Giver of the Light and trapped them somehow inside this structure. There was light, but T'mal felt no heat. He was afraid. Even T'kar, who feared nothing, felt distressed. These humans were somehow able to make the sounds of the people's speech. Perhaps they would explain these strange things to him. T'mal looked from his spear to the lights inside the structure. The spear seemed suddenly inadequate.

The dark human stopped just ahead of them. There was an opening in the solid surface that was all around them. Beyond the opening was another chamber. The dark human entered it, and they followed.

T'mal stopped. There was another human in the chamber, one with a mane on its face, a male. This human male sat before . . . *what was it?* Could it be a weapon of some kind?

T'mal raised his spear, and the human with the mane on his face made motions with his hands, touching the thing before him. T'mal heard the sound of the people's speech, although he was not certain where it came from.

"There is no threat here. This is . . . a thing humans have made so that we can speak to the people. That is its purpose, to help us speak to the people, just as the purpose of your spear is to help you hunt for food. It is only a tool. There is no threat."

T'mal relaxed slightly, then another human came into the chamber. Only this was not a human! It was one of the people . . . but it was not one of the people. The female had a mane just like the manes of the people. The female had eyes just like the eyes of the people. The female had skin . . . almost like that of the people. And within this female, T'mal sensed Ones Who Were! Was this one of the *others*?

"This human female is called Shelby, and she is merged. She is not like any other human. She is . . . other than human. I am called Sean. I am a human Great Father. We have learned to make the sounds of the speech of the people, and we have learned a way for the people to speak to us. There is no threat. Observe this."

The human called Sean spoke in human speech to the dark human. The dark human picked up several things and showed them to T'mal.

"This human is called Paul. What Paul is holding is another thing that we have made. The purpose of this thing is to enable the Ones Who Were to speak to us. This is a tool. Paul will show how this tool is used."

The dark human took the tool and placed it upon his head.

"This tool"—the human called Sean pointed at the tool the dark human had placed on his head—"speaks to this tool." Sean pointed at the thing before him. "With these two tools together, we can hear the Ones Who Were and understand. There is no pain. There is no sensation."

T'mal approached the dark human.

"You must sit down here," the human called Sean indicated the place. "Paul will place this tool upon your head. There is no threat; there is no pain."

Cautiously, T'mal sat down and allowed the tool to be placed upon his head. The other watched, ready to act if there was pain. Sean was making many motions with the very large tool.

"Speak to us as you speak to the Ones Who Were," said Sean.

T'mal did not understand this. He spoke to Great Father T'kar.

"How can the Ones Who Were speak to the humans?" T'mal asked.

"There is much more here than can be understood," T'kar said.

"The One That Is perceives no threat," said T'mal, "but how can tools speak to other tools?"

"Their tools can speak," T'kar said.

"The One That Is does not understand. . . ."      ". . . does not understand. . . ."

T'mal started. The sound of his own speech had filled the chamber suddenly. The young male he had brought with him became very agitated, glancing from T'mal to the humans and back.

"How do you make my speech?" T'mal asked, hearing his own words out loud even as he spoke them internally. It was frightening.

"The tool upon your head can hear you," Sean told him through the larger tool, speaking without using his mouth, but by making motions with his fingers upon the tool before him. "Hearing you, it speaks . . . it speaks without sound to this tool, telling it what you have said. This tool . . . has a way of telling this other tool"—he pointed—"how to make the sounds of your speech. It also tells me what you have said in my speech. It does this without sound. I can look here and see what you have said."

The human looked agitated and spoke to the strange female beside him. Then:

"I know this is hard to understand. I can make this tool hear your speech and . . . make the sounds of your speech in the sounds of human speech. The next words you say to us, you will hear in the sounds of human speech, so that we can understand you."

"The tool will make my speech human speech?" said T'mal, and at the same time heard the sounds of human speech filling the chamber.

"What you heard is your speech, in the sounds of our speech," Sean told him. "I will make this tool say your speech in the sounds of your speech, so that this other male with you can hear and understand."

"You have great power," said T'mal.

"We have much knowledge," said Sean. "It is different from your knowledge."

"Knowledge is power."

"Yes. Knowledge is power. And we have much knowledge. How are you called?"

"T'mal."

"Is there anything you wish to know, T'mal?"

"There is much to know. Why is the human called Paul with skin that is not like yours?"

"Some humans have skin like Paul's. Some have skin like mine. Some have . . . other skin. All are humans. It is how we are."

"I have seen different manes on humans. There is, then, different skin. Do any humans have skin like the people?"

"No."

"Do any humans have eyes like the people?"

"No."

"What is this female?"

"Shelby was once human."

"She is no longer human?"

"She is both of our people and of your people. And she is of neither."

"Is this because she killed to take the Ones Who Were who are within her?" T'mal said.

"She did not kill. A long time ago, she found one of the people who was dying, attacked by a hellhound. She sought, not knowing how, to give comfort to this one. She bore the Touch, not knowing what it was."

"Why do you kill the people?" said T'mal.

"We do not kill the people," Sean told him. "The people attacked us and killed two of us. Why?"

"Humans kill the people. Take the Ones Who Were. Many die the true death. The people must fight. The people must come together. There is another Need now. A Need to drive out the humans. A Need to live."

At sunrise, the Shades brought Jake and Fannon back to the base. Neither of them had been able to get any sleep at all. When they had left with the Shades, they had been marched a short distance from the base to where the Shades had made an impromptu camp of sorts. It was a difficult night. The Shades did not make fire. When the sun went down and the forest was plunged into darkness, Jake and Fannon had not been able to see much past the tips of their noses. The Shades, however, saw quite well in the dark. Fannon and Jake had sat together on the ground, surrounded by a circle of glowing violet eyes. Several times during the night, the Shades had been attacked by hellhounds, which were either killed or driven off. Shortly following the first such attack, one of the Shades came up to them and offered them raw hellhound meat. They had taken the meat, but neither of them felt very hungry. Both men were tired and very much relieved when what Fannon termed "the prisoner exchange" was made at sunrise.

They found out what Sean and Shelby had learned over strong cups of morning coffee.

"This Shade, T'mal," said Sean, "has been somewhat successful in gathering a group of other Shades around him. There aren't very many of them. What you saw last night was it, and it's taken him years just to achieve that. It's a momentous achievement when you consider the fact that it's against their nature to congregate in times other than mating periods and the fact that essentially they are totally unable to communicate with one another. He was thrilled at the idea of the other Shade's being able to hear him through the transducer linkup with the computer and the synthesizer. We've got something that he wants there, and that's a bargaining point."

"Great," said Jake, "but why did they attack us?"

"It's what we thought it was," said Shelby. "The other humans have been attacking them and killing them."

"The ones in that village," said Fannon.

"I'm afraid it's a lot more disturbing than that," said Sean. "According to T'mal, the village that the shuttle spotted is just *one* village. There are many more. From what T'mal told us, I estimate that there are literally *thousands* of humans on Boomerang."

"That's insane," said Jake.

"Shades don't lie," said Shelby. "Even if they did, what would T'mal stand to gain by lying to us?"

"Why haven't we seen them?" said Fannon.

"Well, for one thing," said Sean, "We've confined ourselves pretty much to the base and to this area, fearing to disturb the Shades, at least until we managed to find a way of communicating with them. For another, most of these other humans seem to be on the other side of the mountain range from us. It's only recently that they've started spreading to this side of the continent."

"This is crazy," Fannon said. "*Thousands* of humans on Boomerang?"

"Maybe not so crazy," Jake said. "It bears out our theory about their being the survivors of a ghosting accident. If a ship somehow managed to become marooned in a time before the invention of Zone technology, they would have had *years* in which to become established here. And as the years went by, they gradually reverted, going native. It's imperative that the Directorate be informed of this as soon as possible."

"But what you're saying would mean that there were humans present on Boomerang during the first survey mission," Fannon said. "And, dammit, we didn't *see* any of them!"

"You also confined most of your explorations to this side of the continent," said Paul. "Also, you weren't looking for them."

"But we did make an aerial reconnaissance of the areas we did not explore," said Fannon, "and there was no trace of any 'human villages.'"

"Then they must have been camouflaged," said Sean.

"You're out of your mind."

"It's the only possible explanation," Sean said. "Besides, you haven't heard the rest of it."

"You mean there's more?"

"Lots more. T'mal told us a very chilling story. He was very young when he saw these humans for the first time. It took place during the time of Need, in that canyon up in the mountains. The humans waited until things were well under way, then they stormed the canyon in force. T'mal insisted that they were able to cause pain from a distance."

"Stun rifles?" said Jake.

Sean shook his head. "I thought of that and pressed him on it. They were armed with weapons not much more sophisticated than what the Shades have. What T'mal was describing sounds very much like a psionic attack, *en masse*. A coordinated psionic attack."

"You're talking telepathy."

"I'm talking telepathy. What's more, the entire purpose of this assault was to segregate Shades and kill them, forcing them to choose btween what they call the 'true death' and merging with their attackers. In short, the sum total of what we learned from our conversation with T'mal is that these humans have been here for a very long time indeed, that they have been systematically killing Shades in order to assimilate their Ones Who Were, that they seem to have developed telepathic abilities, that they have been breeding like rabbits so that they are now in competition with the Shades in an environment that will not support them both. In other words, gentlemen, they are committing genocide upon the Shades. And the Shades, no matter how you slice it, don't seem to stand a ghost of chance against them."

# CHAPTER FOURTEEN

"I don't understand it," said Fannon. "I just don't understand it."

Shortly following the meeting with T'mal, they had programmed the ship to make an aerial reconnaissance from orbit. They sat watching as the pictures were transmitted to the screen from aboard the *Wanderer*. There were several villages on their side of the mountain range. On the other side of the continent, the landscape was liberally dotted with settlements. And there were several others under construction.

"It's crazy," Fannon said. "I see it, but I just can't believe it!"

"They've been there all this time," said Shelby.

"And they've been hiding," Sean said.

"Fannon's right," said Paul. "It simply doesn't make sense. While it would certainly take no great effort to hide small settlements from a casual orbital surveillance, the question is, why would they do it?"

"Perhaps they were fearful of discovery by some other, possibly hostile race capable of space travel," Shelby suggested.

"That might make sense," said Fannon, "*if* the settlements were still camouflaged. But they're not, as you can plainly see. It's as if all of a sudden they've whipped the covers off, as if to jump up and down and say, 'Here we are, here we are.' It's crazy!"

"One would think that they knew we were coming and have waited until now to reveal their presence," Shelby said.

"Not necessarily," said Sean. "They could have spotted the *Wanderer* in orbit at some point after our arrival and deduced it was a ship. And, hoping for rescue, they . . . no, that doesn't make much sense, either."

"You mean why didn't they come looking for us?" said Paul.

"They might have, but it's a big planet," said Sean. "I mean, how would they know it was a ColCom ship?"

"We were on our way to that village when the Shades arrived," said Fannon. "I say we pick up where we left off and fly on out there. Let's see what the hell this is all about. Either way, we're going to look like a prize pack of idiots when this is reported to the Directorate."

"I'm not so much concerned with how we're going to appear before the Directorate as I am with our responsibilities in this case," said Paul. "It's been clearly established that a human colony on Boomerang would have a disastrous effect upon the Shades. We now have very dramatic proof of that. And since these people have been here for a very long time, they must now quite obviously regard Boomerang as their home. How do we take sides?"

"I think you should go to the village," Shelby said, "and learn what you can. I'll stay here with Sean and continue working with T'mal and his people. Something is very wrong here, and we've got to find a way to resolve it."

"What do you mean?" said Jake.

"I mean that T'mal said the humans are killing the Shades for their Ones Who Were," said Shelby. "I can understand how that might happen, better than anybody else. It happened to me. If, at some point in the past, one of them or more became merged in the same manner I did, then I can well understand their desire for the communion with the Ones Who Were. What I *can't* understand is how the Ones Who Were who have already become merged into those people can condone the killing. *Why didn't they stop it?*"

"Well, there's only one way we're ever going to find out," said Fannon.

"I think we should go right now," said Jake.

"No," said Fannon. "*I* should go. I'll take Brock and Bascomb with me. If anything goes wrong, you've got to stay behind, Jake. You're going to have to make that trip back to see the Directorate."

"What makes you think anything will go wrong?" said Jake.

"As I said before," said Fannon, "in the field, there's no such thing as being too paranoid. And there's been some talk that the people might have developed esper abilities. If that's true, I'm hardly going to be able to hide the fact that we've been consorting with their enemies."

146

"I think I should go with you, Fannon," Paul said.

Fannon stared at him for a long moment.

"I think you should, too," he said.

The shuttle landed in the center of the village. Within seconds, it was surrounded by people. Humans. They looked as though they had stepped out of Earth's prehistory, dressed in animal skins, carrying primitive weapons, their hair and beards long and shaggy. The only difference was that they were modern humans, not Neanderthals. Little children capered outside the shuttle, leaping up and down and shaking little spears. Everyone was smiling.

The shuttle door opened and Paul and Fannon stepped outside. They all fell silent. A very young, strikingly beautiful female approached them slowly, moving with a stately grace and an air of authority. She came to within arm's reach of them and smiled.

"Drew Fannon," she said. "It's been a very long time."

They sat around a wooden table, on wooden chairs, in a small house that reminded Fannon of the little hunting cabin his father used to lease in Colorado's basement game preserve when he had been a small boy. They drank a slightly bitter brew made from a variety of local berryfruit. It was strong and bestowed a welcome glow. The woman who sat with them looked to be between the ages of fifteen and twenty. She possessed a full figure, but still had the coltishness of youth. The way she was dressed, similarly to the others, reminded Paul of the costume of the early Plains Indians, except that these people stuck to a stark, utilitarian simplicity with no ornamentation. She had long dark hair, which she wore loose; it hung down to her waist.

"It's unnecessary for Andrew Brock and Leila Bascomb to remain inside the shuttle," she said. "You have nothing to fear from us, but if you wish to exercise caution, I have no objection."

"Since it's obviously true that you have fully developed esper abilities," said Fannon, "you also obviously know everything I'm going to ask before I ask it."

She nodded. "Please try not to feel ill at ease," she said. "We can refrain from reading you just as you can refrain from speaking should you choose to, but I think it will be simpler this way. I know what you want to know. It's a very long story.

"We've known of your presence here for quite some time.

147

I even knew you were coming. But I'll get back to that. My name is Lani. I was named after an important member of our tribe. And, like the Shades, we possess Ones Who Were. We've been on Boomerang for about a thousand years now. There were five thousand of us at first. Our ship was destroyed. We established a colony here and began to expand. Over the years, we developed the ability to merge by absorbing Shade entities into ourselves. Our esper abilities also developed. They bred true, since all of the original settlers here had esper potential to some extent. And in answer to the question that just crossed your mind, Drew, yes, Shelby probably has the ability to merge as well. That was passed on to us immediately, although our Touch became stronger over the years. I know about Shelby Michaels, of course, and I'm very anxious to meet her. I also know that you've found a way to communicate with the Shades. I hope you'll share this with us. We would very much like to be able to communicate with them as well. They resist telepathic contact; we've tried many times. When we attempt to force the issue, it causes them great pain. Some of us have greater esper power than others. I am the strongest, and for this reason and the fact that my human Great Mother was the leader of the original five thousand, I am the senior in authority, if not in physical age as the One That Is.

"You want to know about our killing Shades, committing genocide upon them." She sighed. "There simply was no choice. The Shades as they are right now are doomed to extinction, but in a very real sense, we are not murdering them. They continue to exist within us, as a part of us. Unfortunately, many of them have chosen to die the true death rather than merge with a human. I wish that could somehow have been prevented. What I'm about to tell you is going to come as a great shock to you. And it's because of what I am about to tell you that you must leave immediately following our talk. I have instructed my people not to try to read you, and I believe they will all comply with my wishes, but I cannot take the chance that what I'm going to tell you will become known to them. I'm afraid. For generations, the One That Is within whom the original Great Mother lived, the leader of the original five thousand, has been the only one among our people to know the truth, and it was passed on with the Great Mother.

"Paul, Drew, our coming here was not a ghosting accident, as you have supposed. I am Lani, the One That Is, but I am also Lani the Great Hunter of the Ones Who Were. I am

148

Mary, the Great Healer, and S'utar, who was Great Healer before Mary, and D'ali, the Shade Father Who Walked in Shadow, and all the Shade and human entities that are a part of me. I am Drew, the Great Father, who was named for you, Fannon, and I am Great Mother Wendy Chan, who was sent here by the Directorate of ColCom."

As she watched the stunned reactions of both men, tears began to flow down her cheeks.

"I've had a thousand years in which to figure it all out," she said. "And a lot of the missing information I can perceive within your minds. I was cured of my withdrawal and placed into a cryogen aboard a ship called the *Blessing*. Yes, Paul, it was the very ship that was at Gamma 127 when you arrived there. On board that ship were five thousand people, all in coldsleep. All of them must have been carefully selected by ColCom, although I don't know how, nor do I know if their consent was ever given. We were conditioned in coldsleep, programmed by the Directorate to act according to their wishes. Brainwashed, if you will. When we arrived here, we had little in the way of free will. We had to carry out our programming. We were to force Shades to merge with us so that we would inherit their abilities. It must have been hoped that our esper potential would breed true, as it has.

"In order to prevent the Ones Who Were who were absorbed by us from fighting us, we were programmed to believe that we were sent here by the All Father, that we were acting according to His wishes. The idea was for us to believe that we had come from the stars, brought to Boomerang by the All Father so that we would transform the people, the Shades, into a greater race. We were the Seedlings, the instrument of the Lord. Through blood, the Shades would be transformed. This was and is our faith, our religion. None of the people here know anything of Earth or the Directorate or the other colonies, with the exception of myself. They all believe, as they were meant to believe, that they are God's children, on a holy task.

"The Directorate needed me to ghost the ship to Boomerang. It was so important to them that they took the risk of playing with time. I was programmed, I believe, with certain information that would enable me to create the reality of Boomerang some thousand years before I ever first set foot on this world as a member of the original survey team. But once I arrived, it was necessary for me to exert a certain influence upon the experiment.

"If the Shades had already been exposed to humans when

149

the first survey team arrived, history would have been changed, a time paradox created. This had to be avoided. This was facilitated by the fact that Shades are intensely territorial. They seldom venture out of their own domains and have no contact with each other. This has now been changed, I know, because of our activities. We had to settle originally in an area as far removed from that covered by the survey team as possible, so we came to the place where our original settlement still stands. People still live there, beyond the mountains, on the other side of the continent. I had to know about the original survey team, of which I was a part, so that I could make certain that the Shades you would have contact with and you, yourselves, would know nothing of our presence here. I had to know when you would come, so I could arrange for the settlements to be hidden from the ship's cameras. And I had to know when you would leave, so that I would know the time for us to spread beyond the mountains. This meant that certain elements of my programming would have had to wear off or something, so I could have access to information that the others did not have. Just knowing that I was programmed helped me to fight free of it over the years.

"I couldn't tell the others. It would have been disastrous. And I myself did not fully realize our situation for a long, long time. I can't begin to tell you what it felt like when the survey team arrived, knowing that you were there, that I was there, and that I could do nothing without risking dire consequences. The Shade entities within me know the truth and understand it. It causes them tremendous pain. I cannot expose the others to this pain. I can't stop it. The others are all programmed through their Ones Who Were, through our religion and instilled belief. There are too many of us now. The Shades must become absorbed into us or they must die. Either way, it will not be long before the Shades as you know them will cease to exist and only we will remain. The only question that remains is, *why*? And it doesn't take very much intelligence to figure out the answer to that."

"They wanted immortality," Paul whispered. "The plague drug didn't give it to them, so they found another way to achieve it."

Fannon licked his lips and took a deep breath. "You'll have to excuse my ignorance, Doc. I'm still shook up from what I've just heard. I'm afraid I don't get it."

"They sent these people back into Boomerang's past," said Paul, "to conduct a horrifying experiment. That's why Jake and I are supposed to take the *Wanderer* back. Once a year

150

for us, every couple of weeks or so for them. They'll be hearing our reports. If we report, as we were going to, that we've found humans on Boomerang, they would know they had succeeded. Succeeded in creating their own master race. And then they would come for them. Just as these people have been absorbing Shades, so they would be absorbed into the human race, in the hopes of eventually transforming it, mutating it into a race of full espers who possessed the ability to merge and live forever. It might be a wonderful thing for the human race, but I can't believe the end justifies the means."

"I'm afraid for my people," said Lani. "This is our home now. We don't want to leave. I have no idea how the others would react if they were suddenly to discover that they are not God's children, but the result of an experiment in genetics to be harvested like so much wheat."

"Jesus," said Fannon.

"What are you going to do?" said Lani.

Fannon reached for his communicator. "Brock?"

*"Everything all right there?"* Brock replied.

"No. No, everything is not all right. But sit tight, we're okay. We're going to be leaving shortly." He glanced at Lani. "And we're bringing someone with us. Lani, can you tell your people that you're going to come with us and that you'll return in a while?"

She smiled. "The shuttle that brought us down from the *Blessing* before it was destroyed still remains at the original settlement. It's a sacred shrine. They won't be concerned if I leave with you. They'll think of it as a holy pilgrimage."

"I wonder if we'll ever stop advancing our own selfish interests in God's name," murmured Paul.

"What's that?" said Fannon.

"Never mind. Let's get out of here."

Lani's arrival created quite a stir at the base. Everyone wanted to question her, but she was kept away from the personnel until the base leaders could sit down and decide upon a plan of action. Jake and the others heard her incredible story in a private meeting. Then she was taken by Brock and Bascomb to some quarters that had been made available for her while they talked it over.

"I'm afraid I find it incumbent upon myself to play devil's advocate," said Sean. "I find what the Directorate has done detestable, to say the least, and as you said, Paul, the end does not justify the means. However, the means is a *fait accompli* now and we must concern ourselves with the end. The experiment *has* been successful. Its fruits *would* prove a tremendous boon to humanity."

"What are you saying, Sean?" said Shelby. "That we should inform the Directorate that their project has been successful so that they can come and take these people? You know what would happen to them. They would be put to death so they could merge with other humans."

"And I'll bet I know just who the first four candidates for merging are," said Fannon. "Director Anderson and company."

"Sean, you can't seriously mean—" Jake began.

"Hear me out. This is something we *have* to consider," said Sean. "To begin with, these people would not truly die, any more than the Ones Who Were died when they merged with you, Shelby. They will only experience physical death, and there is every reason to believe that this will be made as painless as possible. They are people, after all. They will be forced to merge, true, but they will live on in other bodies. Also, they need not be taken from Boomerang while still young. A sizable number of them will have to remain here, to provide a breeding stock ColCom can draw on. All emotional considerations aside, we have to consider how this situation might proceed. Lani used the term 'harvesting.' All right, let's call it that. Only the old ones need be harvested. And the process will have to be conducted carefully, so there will be a continuity of Ones Who Were to be passed on to those who are born."

"And what about the Shades?" said Shelby.

"Lani has already given us the answer to that question," Sean said. "Their race, as we know it, is in the process of becoming extinct. Or, let's say, becoming transformed. We can't stop the killing. It's become an intergral part of the experiment and of these people's belief system."

"There is one thing you're overlooking," Paul said, "speaking of their belief system. Leaving aside this Nazi ideal of a super race which has an ugly way of resurfacing throughout our history, these people have been conditioned to believe that they have been sent to Boomerang by the Shade deity, the All Father. They believe this deity to be real, to be *their* deity. The existence of a supreme-being archetype is already extant in human nature; we are all born with a predisposition to it. The Directorate merely strengthened and redirected it to suit their own purposes. What happens when they find out the truth? What happens when they learn that it was not a god who sent them here on some holy mission, but men with a cold and ruthless purpose? Remember that we're dealing with gestalt personalities composed of hundreds of thousands of entities. What happens when they're all subjected to such a shock?"

"It would be a risk, to be sure," said Sean, "but you yourself have pointed out in the past that a personality such as Shelby's has the potential, if not actually realized, of an almost perfect integration. The Ones Who Were are motivated by a tremendous instinct for survival. When Shelby merged with her Shade, those Ones Who Were experienced a traumatic shock resulting from their merging with an alien being. It caused Shelby some great problems, true, but she has survived and found a strong stability in what she has become. Consider why a person with your training was sent here, Paul. Was it to study the behavior of Shades, when a xenobiologist would seem eminently more qualified for the job? We already have several such here. It happens to be one of my own special fields of study. Was it to observe the personnel here, to provide therapy in the event of problems created by our situation? Very possibly, but I submit to you that a person with qualifications not quite so impressive as yours could have performed that job admirably. Or was it to observe Shelby Michaels, to all intents and purposes the control in this experiment? Was it to enable you to study and observe the Seedlings, to see how the experiment has affected them? Such a task would require someone who was more than merely a superb psychiatrist. It would require a highly trained member of the SEPAP corps."

"Did you *know* about this all along?" said Fannon.

"Don't be absurd, you idiot, of course I didn't know! I'm hardly that important. I've merely made some very logical deductions, which if you were thinking with your brain instead of with your gut, you'd be able to make as well."

"So you think this is all for the collective good of all mankind?" said Paul.

"I'm not making any value judgments," Sean said. "I'm merely asking you to consider them. Because you're going to have to make them. You might be able to keep this information from the Directorate for a time, but for how long? Suppose they decide to wire you for a debriefing? Not an inconsistent procedure, as you well know. And that's only the simplest method of their finding out; there are others. You can't keep this from them. And I don't think you can stop them, either."

"We can try," said Fannon.

"And what are you going to accomplish?" Sean said. "Are you going to be able to save the remaining Shades? How? By turning on your own kind? Even if you made such an insane decision, which I don't think it's in you to make, they vastly outnumber us. We have the superior technology, because they have been conditioned to remain in a backward state for the sake of convenience, but what would you do with it? If you find it abhorrent that the Seedlings are committing genocide upon the Shades, would you find it any less abhorrent to commit genocide upon the Seedlings? Could you kill *Wendy*, Fannon? Because Lani *is* Wendy. And what's the alternative, to fight the Directorate? How? We're just a handful of people here. And we all want to go home."

"So what are you suggesting, Sean?" said Jake quietly.

"I'm saying that there's nothing we can do about it," Sean said. "And I'm trying to suggest a way for us to be able to sleep nights. We're not responsible for this. We just got caught smack in the middle. We're the victims, too."

"Is that what you're going to tell T'mal next time he comes?" said Shelby bitterly.

Sean put his head in his hands. "Damn," he said. *"Damn!"* He took a deep breath and let it out slowly. "There is one thing we *can* tell him. We can perpetuate the lie told by the Directorate. Convince him and his people that we *have* been sent by the All Father. Convince him not to fight the Seedlings. At least that way maybe we can save some Shades from choosing the true death."

"And what do we tell Lani?" Fannon said.

"Great Mother Wendy is the strongest of the Seedlings," Sean said. "And she was your fellow survey officer."

"I see," said Fannon. "I know her best and so I get the dirty work. I get to tell her that we're just victims, too, is that it?"

"Do we have any other choice?" said Sean.

"You know, I knew you had a nasty temper, McEnroe," said Fannon. "But until now, I didn't know you were a bastard."

He closed the door behind him softly. Lani stood as he entered. She looked at him for a moment, then sighed and looked down at the floor. Fannon approached her.

"I was wondering what in hell I was going to say to you," he said. "I forgot that I wouldn't have to *say* anything. I'm—"

"I know you're sorry," she said. She sat down on the bed, looking very small.

"I don't know what to do," said Fannon.

She shrugged. "Don't feel bad, Drew. I understand."

"You must really hate me."

She smiled. "How can I hate you, Drew? I'm still Wendy, remember? I named my first child after you. I loved you. I always have. I knew you would come back. Maybe, deep down inside, I also knew that there would be nothing you could do."

"Lani . . ."

"Call me Wendy, Drew. I may not look the same, but I'm still me."

"And a host of others, too."

"But I'm still *me*. You found that hard to accept with Shelby, too, didn't you?"

"Dammit, Wendy, I wish to hell you'd stop reading my mind!"

"I can't help it, Drew. You still feel something for me, don't you? I know you find me beautiful."

"You're just a child."

"I'm over a thousand years old, Drew. And I've been carrying this around with me all that time. It took many, many years to fight off all that conditioning, but I still knew what would happen to us. I don't know what I'm going to tell my people, Drew. It hurts. It hurts so much. They've done such an awful thing to us."

She was weeping. He put his arm around her, and she buried her head against him, sobbing quietly.

"We never had a chance, did we?" she said. "I wish to God we'd never even met."

"Wendy, please . . ."

"Make love to me, Drew? Let's just not talk about it anymore. Make love to me just as you used to, a thousand years ago."

She looked up at him, face wet with tears.

"Please?"

Their lips met, and they sank down onto the bed.

# CHAPTER FIFTEEN

Jake Thorsen came awake with the feeling that there was someone in his room. He smelled cigarette smoke.

"Fannon?"

He was instantly alert. He turned on the light. Fannon was sitting at Jake's desk, dressed in a robe.

"What's wrong?"

"You're slipping, son," Fannon said. "I've been here at least five minutes."

Jake sat up in bed, frowning.

"I've been sitting here and thinking," Fannon said, "trying to figure out just what to say to you. I'm still not sure."

"You want a drink?"

"Yes, thanks."

Jake got up, dressed only in his shorts, and walked across the room to get the bottle of Scotch.

"Forget the glasses."

"All right."

He handed the bottle to Fannon, who took it, removed the cap, and took a long pull.

"I want to stop it, Jake. It's gone too far. The whole fucking thing is crazy, and I want to stop it."

Jake took the bottle and had a drink. "I'm listening."

"Remember once, a long time ago, we talked about using the *Wanderer* to ghost our way out of here?"

"Yes."

"We can't go forward, not without probably killing ourselves, but we can go back, Jake. Way back. ColCom has proved it can be done. Wendy did it. We can figure out a way to go back before this whole thing started and stop it that way."

"How?"

"I've been thinking about that. We can go back to when

156

the first survey team was here. The Directorate would never have known about the Shades if we hadn't—"

"Hold it right there," said Jake.

"What?"

"You're not thinking. The Directorate went to a lot of trouble to avoid a paradox. You're talking about deliberately creating one. You're talking about changing the past, Fannon. It can't be done."

"They did it."

"By going around the paradox. We can't do that. In order to accomplish what you're talking about, you'd have to go back into the past and meet yourself. And I'd have to go back with you, because you can't pilot the *Wanderer*, certainly not alone. Suppose, since we're talking about crazy things here, that you were able to go back into the past and meet yourself. How would you stop yourself from doing what you've already done? Would you prevent Shelby from having become merged? Even if you could, you know what you would be condemning her to. You remember what she was like before. Suppose that you were able to change things. What reason would the Directorate have then for sending you back to Boomerang? If you acted in the past in any way differently from the way you had, you probably would not be here now. I would not be here now. The *Wanderer* would not be here nor any of those other people. You're talking about the grandfather paradox, Fannon."

"So you won't do it?"

"I *can't* do it. And if you think about it, you'll realize I'm right."

"So what's the answer, then? To do it Sean's way?"

"Sean's way is the logical way," said Jake. "That doesn't mean it's the right way, but what *is* the right way?"

"At least, at the very least, we owe T'mal the truth," said Fannon.

"Then the Shades will continue to fight," said Jake.

"God knows, they've got a right to."

"They'll lose. It's inevitable. And knowing the truth, they'll doubtless opt for the true death."

"They've got a right to do that, too."

"Sean was right, you know," said Jake. "We're the victims, just as much as they are. Sometimes you have no choice. Sometimes you just have to stand by and watch things happen that you can't condone. You have to because you can't do anything about it."

"I can't accept that," said Fannon.

"It's a very hard thing to accept."

"Well, I'm not going to do it," Fannon said. He took another long pull from the bottle. It was almost half empty. "The damn Rhiannon thing's come back to haunt me again. I knew I should've quit after that. This time, they've finally found a 'cost-effective' way to wipe out a whole race. Eminently practical. Very logical. And they don't even die, not really. Well, we might lose a few here and there, but it's of no consequence, right? And when it comes to the Seedlings being used as breeding stock, well, think of the benefit to mankind. Who could possibly object?"

He rose unsteadily to his feet. "I'm taking the bottle with me," he said, and left.

In the morning, they skipped first mess and met in the lab. Sean made coffee. Fannon came in with Lani.

"I don't think that—" Sean began.

"What difference could it possibly make, Sean?" said Lani.

"Yes, of course," said Sean. "You're quite right. There's little point in our trying to keep anything from you."

"We've got to tell our people something," Jake said. "They've got a right to know what's happening."

"What are we going to tell them, Jake?" said Paul. "Have we decided on a course of action?"

"I thought I made it pretty clear last night that we don't have much in the way of options," Sean said.

"We do have one," said Shelby, standing in the doorway.

Lani looked up at her, smiled sadly, and looked away.

"We don't have to go back," said Shelby. She looked at Jake. "You don't have to go back with Paul. Without someone who's been to Boomerang to ghost a ship for them, they would have to use sublight drive to get here."

"Well, yes, that's true," said Sean. "But they would get here eventually. I don't see how that would help the Shades or Lani's people."

"It would at least buy them some time," said Shelby.

"That still won't make the situation here any easier," said Sean. "And what about *our* people?"

"He's right," Paul said. "There isn't anybody here who hasn't been nurturing the hope that they will someday be allowed to leave. You're asking them to spend the rest of their lives here with no possible hope of ever going back."

"But Lani's people—"

"Yes, we could absorb them when the time comes for them to die," said Lani. "But our way of life is different. It would

158

be hard for them. And sooner or later, ColCom would come for them as they will come for us."

"Your solution is no solution, Shelby," Sean said. "It would only be delaying the—"

There was a knock at the door.

"Yes?"

The door opened and Brock entered. "T'mal is here with one of the other—"

T'mal and another Shade were just behind Brock in the open doorway. At the sight of Lani, T'mal lunged forward, shoving Brock out of the way. In an instant, even as Lani was leaping to her feet, T'mal's spear was hurtling across the room. Reacting with astonishing speed, Fannon hurled himself at Lani, pushing her out of the way. As quickly as he had moved, he hadn't moved quickly enough. Lani fell to the floor from the force of his shove, and T'mal's spear penetrated Fannon's stomach with the sound of a knife being plunged into a grapefruit.

Brock and the other man with him fired, and both T'mal and the second Shade crumpled to the floor. Shelby cried out Fannon's name and was at his side in an instant.

Sean grabbed Brock, furiously slamming him against the wall.

*"You fucking brainless idiot! What have you done?"*

All the color had drained from Brock's face. "I thought—I didn't know—"

Lani bent over T'mal. "He's dead," she said. The charges fired had been lethal. Both Shades were finished.

Fannon was half sitting on the floor, being supported by Paul and Shelby. The spear had gone in through his stomach with such force that it now protruded from his back. Fannon was breathing horribly, his face contorted. Jake took the spear and began to pull it out, but Fannon cried out and clasped the shaft of the spear with both hands.

"Leave it," he choked out. "I've bought it."

Lani moved toward him, then glanced at Shelby and hesitated. Shelby looked up at her, panic-stricken.

*"Do it! Do it, you can save him!"*

Lani shook her head. "No. You want him more than I do. You take him."

"But I *can't!* I don't know—"

"You *can*. You know you can."

Shelby felt her in her mind. The Ones Who Were took over, supported by the strength of all of Lani's personality. She *could* do it. She became very calm.

"I knew I should've quit after Rhiannon," Fannon said, between rasping breaths. "Oh, *shit*, it hurts!" He gasped.

"Drew, look at me," said Shelby.

*"Do it quickly,"* Lani said in her mind.

"No . . . don't. Let me . . ."

She Touched him.

Directors Anderson, Jorgensen, Hermann, and Malik entered the wardroom of the *Wanderer*. A week and a half had gone by for them on orbital station Gamma 127 since they had last seen Colonel Jake Thorsen, since they had sent Dr. Paul Tabarde to Boomerang. Jake and Paul were already seated at the wardroom table, waiting for them.

"Colonel Thorsen, Doctor," said Anderson. "It's good to see you gentlemen again. And how are things on Boomerang?"

"Interesting, to say the least," said Jake.

"Well, we're all anxious to hear the details," said Director Malik.

"I think you'll find this very interesting," said Jake. Then he raised his voice. "Shelby?"

Shelby entered the wardroom with Lani. The effect of Lani's appearance on the four men was electric.

"This young woman's name is Lani," said Jake. "She is part of a very large and rapidly growing human colony on Boomerang. In fact, she's their leader. But you gentlemen would already know that, wouldn't you, since you sent her there when she was Lieutenant Wendy Chan."

"My God, it's worked," said Anderson. "It's worked!"

"Yes, the Seedling project has been a resounding success," said Shelby. "But it stops right here."

Malik frowned. "What do you mean, it stops right here? Colonel Michaels, I don't think you—"

"For the moment, Captain Drew Fannon," Shelby said.

They stared at her. *"Fannon?"* said Hermann.

"Yes, Fannon. I had a little accident, you might say. Caught a spear in my gut. Frankly, I think I'd rather it had ended there, but Shelby had other ideas. It's a moot point, now."

"You merged with her!" said Anderson. "Splendid! And Lani has all these abilities as well?"

"Oh, yes. And then some," Fannon said through Shelby.

"This is wonderful!" said Anderson. "Do you realize what this means? It's the answer to our prayers! You'll all be able to come home now. You'll be heroes, every one of you! This moment will go down in history as humanity's greatest triumph! We have beaten death! Think of it! It's stupendous!"

"No more death from fatal diseases," said Jorgensen. "New hope for the plague children. A new dawn for the entire human race!"

"Before you get too carried away with patting yourselves on the back," said Shelby/Fannon, "I think you should know that history will remain completely ignorant of this 'stupendous' moment."

"What are you talking about?" said Anderson.

"Simply that the human race is going to have to be content with remaining mortal for a while," Jake said. "We've decided not to allow you to go through with it."

"*You've* decided? Tabarde, what in heaven's name is this all about?" said Malik.

"In a way, it's about Rhiannon," Paul said. "It's also about the baby farms of the Third Reich, since you seem to be so concerned with history. And about the plague drug, and countless other forms of insanity. It's about genocide. It's about the repellent idea of sacrifice for the common good. It's about the socialist creed that the end justifies the means."

"What in God's name . . .?" said Anderson.

"No, definitely not in God's name," Paul said. "I think that quite enough has been done in God's name."

"Let's not get excited," said Jorgensen. "We are all rational human beings here—"

"I question that," said Paul.

"Be that as it may," Jorgensen continued, "am I to understand that you people have some idea of *preventing* the culmination of the Seedling project?"

"We don't have 'some idea' of preventing it," said Shelby, "we *are* preventing it."

Jorgensen glanced from one to the other of them and began to chuckle.

"This is truly absurd," he said. "I don't even begin to claim to understand whatever lunacy motivates you in this, but are you seriously suggesting that we deny the human race the greatest gift in all the universe? We have in our hands the power to transform humanity, to make ourselves immortal! This is our destiny! And you are quite powerless to prevent it, though I confess it baffles me completely as to why you should even want to!"

"Not too long ago," said Jake, "I told Fannon that we were victimized, just as you have victimized the Shades, just as you intend to victimize the people whom you so dispassionately refer to as the Seedlings. I told him that there are times when a person has no choice, when it's necessary to stand by and watch helplessly something that you can't condone simply because you are powerless to do anything about it. Fannon would not accept that. And, in my heart, I could not accept it, either. We found that we were not quite as powerless as we thought, that we didn't have to become victims."

"You're not making any sense," said Anderson. "I don't understand—"

"That much is clear to us," said Paul, "that you people really don't understand what it is that you have done. Well, we shall take steps to see that you do understand. Completely."

"Are you *threatening* us?" said Malik.

"If you have some insane idea of doing us some sort of harm," said Hermann, rising to his feet, "you'll never get away with it! This is a ColCom outpost. I warn you that if you attempt any sort of action against us, you and this ship will never—"

*"Sit down and shut up, Hermann!"* shouted Jake.

The man looked shocked. His mouth worked soundlessly and he sat back down.

"I'll tell you precisely what we're going to do," said Jake, "and why we're going to get away with it. In a very short while, the *Wanderer* will depart Gamma 127 for Boomerang. Before we go, however, you gentlemen will have taken certain steps to declassify the Boomerang mission. You will clear the way for all the people there to leave and go anywhere they want to. They've all had a bellyful of the service, and I expect that most if not all of them will be resigning. ColCom records will be quite specific on the subject of Boomerang. The planet is now listed as being unsuitable for colonization. You will change that designation to 'quarantined world.' We can't do anything about what you've already done, but at least the new race that is an amalgam of the Shades and the people whom you've sent there will be able to continue to live their way, in peace."

"You're mad," said Joregnsen. "You can't force us to—"

"But we *can* force you," said Paul. "Your own visionary desires to create a super race have given us that power. Lieutenant Wendy Chan had esper potential. Lani is a full esper and, you will find, a very strong one."

"Even if I did not suspect it," Lani said, "I can see it in your minds. You did not wish to make the same mistake

162

made by the inventors of the plague drug. You did not dare. You have been extremely secretive about the Seedling project from the very start, both to protect yourselves in case it failed and to take all the credit if it succeeded. No one else knows about it except you four. The people on Boomerang know, but those who will be leaving have all volunteered to 'forget' via conditioning. If they are ever questioned about Boomerang, they will have a very different story to tell."

"You see," said Paul, "some people believe that there are more important things than immortality."

"Paul and I will remain behind at Gamma with you," Lani said. "We will go back aboard the station, Paul and myself dressed in service uniforms. I will make sure you carry out our wishes, and then, after the *Wanderer* has departed, we will depart aboard your own ship. We will file a mission plan, but you will never reach your destination."

"You can't *do* this!" Anderson said, but with a brief stab at their minds, Lani told them that she could.

"Surely you don't intend to kill us!" said Hermann, panicking.

"No," said Jake softly. "Not exactly."

"Do you people realize just what it is you're doing?" said Anderson. "You're playing God with the fate of humanity!"

Paul smiled. "How conveniently you throw that concept around," he said. "We're not playing God, any more than you played God with the fate of the Shades, with our fate, and with the five thousand people you brainwashed and sent to Boomerang. You even created your own Christ," said Paul, indicating Lani. "Throughout all her lifetimes, she has had to carry the burden of your sin alone, to follow the analogy. Over a thousand years, she knew; the Ones Who Were within her knew and bore the pain. Christ only had to die once upon the cross."

"What are you going to do with us?" said Anderson fearfully.

"Why, we're going to kill you," Shelby/Fannon said, "but only just a little. You'll be going to Boomerang to behold the fruits of your labors, as long as we're all being so biblical here. Your deaths will be quick and painless, and you will live on as part of Lani, among her Ones Who Were."

"You see, gentlemen," said Paul, "you're going to realize your destiny. You're going to become immortal."

# EPILOGUE

Paul Tabarde looked out the window of his conapt at the Bourbon Street atrium. It felt strange to be back in New Orleans, to see the curious mixture of the old and new as, down below, the Mardi Gras parade snaked its way among the massive support columns of the city while mini-shuttles hovered overhead, showering the people with the traditional doubloons.

The new Directors of ColCom were sharing the honors as Grand Marshals of the festivities. One of them, Viselius, was a horribly deformed plague child who could not get around without a bracing exoskeleton, but in the crowd below, he did not stand out at all among all the outlandish costumes.

Paul had his old job back, and he was happy. It had surprised him how easily he had fallen back into the old SEPAP routine. The endless reports, the daily commute to Colorado—it seemed almost as though he had never left. He had personally handled the disposition of the personnel who returned from Boomerang. His official recommendation, approved by the new Directorate, was that they all be given honorable hardship discharges from the service, with commendations and full pensions as well as assistance in finding new employment. It would not be at all difficult for people with their credentials, in spite of the high unemployment figures. Those who had not returned from Boomerang were listed as DIS, "deceased in service." Paul knew that in the strictest sense, the word "deceased" would never apply to them. Not ever.

A gentle tone alerted him to the fact that he had a visitor. He went to the console and punched up the screen.

"Havin' a party up there, Doc?" asked the security man.

"No, why, Joe?"

The security man winked at him. "Okay, Doc. I understand. You know me, discretion is my middle name. Should I send the lady up?"

The camera panned, and Paul saw a woman with snow-white hair, skin that had a sheen of silvery blue, and startlingly bright violet eyes.

"Happy Mardi Gras, eh, Doc?" said Joe.

Paul smiled. "Please send the lady up, Joe. And see to it that we're not disturbed."

While he was waiting, he fetched a couple of glasses and a bottle of vintage French wine.

"Hello, Paul."

"Shelby! Come, sit, have a drink. I didn't even know you were in town!"

She kissed him on the cheek. "I can only stay for a little while, Paul. I've got to catch the shuttle to the Cheyenne Spaceport tonight."

"Oh, I see. You're going back."

She shook her head. "No, not to Boomerang. I suppose I could get there if I wanted to—buy a small ship, file a flight plan, and have a ghosting 'accident.' Expensive a proposition as that would be, I could afford it on my pension. There's just nothing there for me anymore."

Paul nodded. "Yes, I can understand that. It wouldn't be the same." He thought of Lani. "It's *their* world now. Where will you go?"

She shook her head and shrugged. "I don't know, really. The only places that I know are Boomerang and the control room of a ship. But Drew knows lots of places. We've shared some memories of them, and I think we'll go experience a few of them."

"How's that working out?"

She shifted in her chair; her whole body took on a different attitude, and she gave a dry chuckle.

"Well, I'll tell you, Doc, it's damned strange. I figured on a lot of ways I could end up, but I never dreamed it would be in the body of a woman, sharing consciousness with an alien civilization. What was that ancient Chinese curse? May you live in interesting times?"

Paul laughed. "Still not fully integrated, eh? I knew you'd be independent to the last."

"Well, now, I don't know. This is a very different sort of scene, but there's a lot to recommend it. I find T'lan's not as strange a character as I thought him to be. In some ways, we've got a lot in common."

165

"Ah, yes. The Shadow entity." Paul nodded. "That would follow."

"Once a shrink, always a shrink, eh?"

"A man's gotta do what a man's gotta do."

"Now where have I heard that before? You want to pass anything on to Jake?"

"Is he in town, too?"

"No, we'll be shipping out with him. He's bought himself a commercial freighter and we're hitching a ride to parts unknown."

"Give him my very best."

"Will do." Abrupty, she was Shelby again. But then, she had never stopped being Shelby. "What shall we drink to, Paul?"

"Well, since we've reached an epiphany of sorts, why not to new beginnings?"

She smiled and raised her glass.

"To new beginnings."

# AFTERWORD

Very early in my writing career, I had resolved never to write sequels or a series. Since what you are holding in your hands is a sequel to *Last Communion*, I was obviously as firm in my resolve as I was in giving up smoking, drinking, and wrecking expensive motorcycles. I have never been consistent and I suspect I never will be. Like Charlie Brown (the kid in the comics, not the publisher of *Locus*), I appear to be doomed to a life of wishy-washiness.

Now, I'm sure you've heard writers talking about how every once in a while you happen upon an idea that you simply can't let go, that has too many possibilities for just one book. I've said this myself, when, in fact, it's all a lot of hogwash. I am convinced that *every* idea has too many possibilities for just one book. The trick is to *resist* writing sequels, and this is very difficult to do, for several reasons.

For one thing, the series is a successful literary tradition, as evidenced by the work of writers as diverse as Conan Doyle and Proust. Readers like them. Publishers are always looking for a series. (Very practical people, publishers. They only like what sells, for some strange reason.) A series is fun to do, so why should one bother to resist the temptation? Well, consider the case of Conan Doyle, who became so fed up with Holmes that he tried to toss him over the Reichenbach Falls, only his readers would have none of it. It could take you over, which is a mixed blessing at best. Take Karl Hansen, for example, after whom the Hansen magnets that create the Twilight Zone are named in this story. (Inside joke which you would understand if you ever went drinking with Karl.) Karl wrote a novel called *War Games*. The publisher added the subtitle

"Set in the Hybrid Universe." Now Karl has to write more novels, also "set in the Hybrid Universe." And if he doesn't, *I'll* be pissed off, because I loved *War Games* and want to read more. And therein lies the rub. If it works well, you don't want it to end, and neither does the reader. Now this kind of thing could get out of hand.

I outlined a novel with the working title *Sergeant Knight* and submitted it to a publisher. The publisher asked for three novels. *Three?* But I had only intended to write *one*. On the other hand, I can see where . . . and you're suckered in, trapped, gleefully allowing the idea to take over and run away with you. Believe it or not, I can now see where the idea that led to that novel could easily result in a veritable *cornucopia* of sequels, and I find that frankly frightening.

When I started to write *Last Communion*, I had no idea that there would be a sequel. By the time I was well into it, I already had a fair idea of what the sequel would be about. When I wrote *Fall into Darkness*, I envisioned at least a trilogy, but I liked the ending of it so well that I can't bear to write another word. And I won't. So help me. It can be a lot of fun, but it can make you crazy.

Fun, did I say? I had the temerity to mention to a more experienced writer that I found this fun. Oh, sure, it's lots of fun, he said. A real labor of love. You get out of shape from leading a sedentary life, you develop lower-back pain from hours spent sitting at the typewriter, you get headaches, anxiety attacks, you suffer sleepless nights, you lose your eyesight gradually, you develop forearms like Popeye's (assuming that you use a manual typewriter, as I have always done), on and on he went, ticking off the trials and tribulations of the literary life, and I stood there, nodding my head, getting more and more depressed, wondering why I was doing this instead of selling dope or running guns or any of a number of other activities that are a lot more profitable and seem to entail less hassle.

And I guess what it comes down to is that in spite of all that other stuff, it *is* fun. Really. You're your own boss. You get up when you want to, you go to bed when you want to, you work when you want to. And you get to do what they always punished you for when you were a kid in school. Daydream. You put your dreams on paper and get paid for it in the bargain. And if the readers like it, that makes all that other stuff worthwhile. Long as all you people continue to feel that you're getting your money's worth and keep coming back for more instead of spending the money on a six-pack, I won't mind losing my hair so much.

Now, about those new beginnings ...

Nicholas Yermakov
Merrick, New York

NICHOLAS YERMAKOV was born on September 30, 1951, in New York City. He has been a rock musician, an actor, an armed guard for a private police force in Beverly Hills, a journalist, a factory worker, a motorcycle salesman, a book store clerk, a disc jockey, a bartender, a dishwasher, and a radio production specialist for the United Nations. A fulltime writer, his work has appeared in *Fantasy and Science Fiction, Heavy Metal, Galaxy,* and several anthologies, as well as in several nonfiction publications. He is the author of *Last Communion* (available in a Signet edition), *Journey From Flesh, Fall Into Darkness,* and *Clique.* He and his wife, Keli, make their home in southern California.